The Last Half of the Year

© 2016, Paul Rowe

 Canada Council for the Arts / Conseil des Arts du Canada   Newfoundland Labrador

We gratefully acknowledge the financial support of the Canada Council for the Arts, the Government of Canada through the Canada Book Fund (CBF), and the Government of Newfoundland and Labrador through the Department of Business, Tourism, Culture and Rural Development for our publishing program.

All rights reserved. No part of this work covered by the copyrights hereon may be reproduced or used in any form or by any means—graphic, electronic or mechanical—without the prior written permission of the publisher. Any requests for photocopying, recording, taping or information storage and retrieval systems of any part of this book shall be directed in writing to the Canadian Reprography Collective, One Yonge Street, Suite 1900, Toronto, Ontario M5E 1E5.

Cover Design by Todd Manning • Layout by Joanne Snook-Hann
Printed on acid-free paper

Published by
KILLICK PRESS
an imprint of CREATIVE BOOK PUBLISHING
a Transcontinental Inc. associated company
P.O. Box 8660, Stn. A
St. John's, Newfoundland and Labrador A1B 3T7

Printed in Canada

Library and Archives Canada Cataloguing in Publication

Rowe, Paul, 1954-, author
    The last half of the year / Paul Rowe.

ISBN 978-1-77103-080-9 (paperback)

    I. Title.

PS8635.O885L37 2016   C813'.6   C2016-901102-X

The Last Half of the Year

Paul Rowe

A NOVEL

St. John's, Newfoundland and Labrador, 2016

For DJR

... sad and weary I go back to you, my cold father, my cold mad father ..."

- FINNEGANS WAKE

July

Jasie Dade was born by the sea in a little place called Birthlayn. Where the name came from is something of a mystery. Some say it was inspired by the small boats that make their way into the shelter of the Back Pond through the Little Gut — a *berth* at the end of a watery *lane*. There's a vague legend about a woman who gave birth all alone out on the barachois; or it might have something to do with the endless shorebirds that nest and breed along the narrow stretch of beach, which the locals call the Bar.

The land that rolls in from the sea takes the form of a wide river valley, though the inhabitants of Birthlayn would never describe it that way. Even the words *river* and *valley* are too grand for their little place. The *valley* is just hillsides and evergreens; the *river*, a simple brook. The creatures in the brook are not *fish* but, more properly, *trout* that gather in two briny, weed-filled ponds (not *lakes*) that mark the end of the brook's slow soggy progress from the inland bogs and marshes. The two ponds, divided by a narrow road, are called the Front and Back Pond, and the road itself is simply called the Downs Road because it leads to a broad stretch of meadow called the Downs.

A lot of places and things in Birthlayn hadn't been named anything at all until the generation of youngsters that little Jasie Dade belonged to came along. Like their parents before them, the children were often quite practical in their naming, but sometimes they let their imaginations soar. For instance, they named the bald patch of rock at the eastern tip of the valley the High Mountains, adding to their sense of adventure in trooping up there on hot summer days to pick the raspberries that dangled like surprising rubies amongst the prickly stalks and bright green leaves. They named the brook, as well, by dividing it into sections according to the head of the family whose meadow it happened to cross. The woods were similarly divided up and named so that you suddenly had Mrs. Mary's or Mr. James's Brook and Uncle Paddy's or Mr. Bob's Woods in a place where for generations there'd always been just the one unnamed brook and hillsides covered with unnamed stands of trees. Last names were avoided since practically everyone in Birthlayn, except little Jasie Dade's family, had the surname Breen.

The youngsters, in another imaginative flair, called the woods near the Downs, the Groves, as though it was full of orange and apple trees instead of plain spruce and fir — plus the larch and birch that add a splash of colour in the fall. In the middle of the Groves there was a clearing where, also in little Jasie's time, youngsters began playing softball and field hockey. The Groves became the place where many of those youngsters smoked their first cigarette — bought five for a dime at Breen's store — or had their first sexual experience with a skin mag, or with another boy or girl. Summer days in the Groves were blissful, the air heavy with the smell of evergreens and scented mosses, plus the flowers, shrubs, and grasses that flourished under the youngsters' roaming feet.

One hot July day, Jasie Dade had wandered away from the others when a bird exploded out of the grass with a rush and whirr that sent his little heart skittering into his throat. Once calmed, he approached the spot in narrowing concentric circles until he found what he was looking for — the nest! — neatly concealed under a small grass canopy. It contained four mottled brown eggs. Little Jasie realised he'd found, not just an ordinary sparrow's nest, but one belonging to the exotic shorebirds that inhabited the nearby pond. He picked up one of the eggs. It was warm to the touch and he rolled it in his palm. He saw a tiny hole in one end and held it to his eye. To his amazement, he saw something move.

His cry brought everyone running.

Irresistibly, slowly, with everyone standing silently in attendance, Jasie liberated the thing inside the egg. As each speckled chip fell from his damp fingers, an embryonic creature was revealed; tiny red veins wired through translucent flesh, incipient wings, a yellow mould of beak, dark eyes welded shut, and the softest imaginable layering of down. Lying at last in Jasie's palm, unfurled, the creature opened its beak in what seemed an heroic attempt to fill its virgin lungs with air and, on the exhalation, to perhaps make its first sound. Instead, exhausted by the effort, it collapsed and died.

At the supper table that night, Jasie's older brother Georgie described it all to their father. Saul Dade laid down his fork and looked up from his food. "You shouldn't have done that, Jasie," he said, firmly. "A bird develops its muscles by fighting its way out of the shell. By helping, you killed it. It needed that struggle to survive."

Morning breaks on a brand new July day. Jason Dade picks up the TV remote, snaps off the Indian-head test pattern, and moves to the kitchen table to watch the sun come up over the High Mountains. He sees a lone robin sweep into the yard and hop about, cocking its head here and there to listen for worms. Neat rows of turnip greens and red-veined beet leaves garnish the brown soil in his father's vegetable garden. Young cabbages cradle the morning dew like small glass beads. The potato plants are nearly a foot high already, their leaves palpitating in the merest of summer breezes.

The robin takes to wing when Sarah's pony meanders forlornly into the yard dragging the thick hemp rope that for too long now has been fastened around its neck. Two weeks earlier, Jason had gone down the road with fifty dollars in his hand when the pony came up for sale. His father, ever against even the most common household pets, was not pleased. But the horse has stayed, for Sarah's sake, though Jason knows the old man is simply biding his time to be rid of it.

Bedsprings creak down the hall as the old man rolls out of bed.

Saul Dade has always worked away from home on large mining and hydroelectric projects. Jason has never known his father to make a living from the sea, but in recent weeks he's learned that his father does indeed know, and seems to enjoy, whatever it is men do when they fish together on the ocean in small boats. Jason hears him cross the hall and stir about mysteriously in the bathroom. (Apart from elusive scents and smells, his father has a way of leaving no trace of ever having been in the bathroom at all.) Soon he will come into the kitchen and prepare for his day on the water. The grey plastic lunchbox is packed and ready on the table, the razor-sharp filleting knife clipped into a leather sheath beside it.

Jason glances out the window and, seized by an idea, slips the knife from its sheath and heads out the door.

He approaches the pony, slips the knife under the rope and begins a slow sawing motion. The blade, from years of stropping, curves to a fine point, an exquisite tip which almost touches the watery surface of the eye. Jason sees his own pale face there past the reflection of the moving dark blade. The pony snorts heavily, but doesn't budge. Jason knows what a sudden toss of the pony's head could mean right now — a bloody blade, a ruined eye, a sister's grief, a father's rage — and yet he somehow knows that on this bright new morning the normally impetuous pony will be still — and so she is — until the rope drops harmlessly to the ground. The pony bats long eyelashes at him and, with a coquettish feminine gait, clops casually out of the yard.

There's a rapping on the glass. He turns to see his father beckoning him inside.

"Don't take that knife out of the house again," Saul says, as Jason steps into the kitchen. "I don't want it lost."

He puts out his hand and Jason passes it over, handle first, as his father has taught him always to do with knives.

"The horse was in trouble with the rope."

"The horse is nothing but trouble and should never be here in the first place."

Jason watches the proceedings from the rocking chair that sits under the little "Bless Our House" cardboard crucifix. Saul Dade has on a red plaid work shirt buttoned to the throat and heavy green work pants that are tucked into his rubber boots. He returns the knife to the sheath which he then threads onto his belt, plugs in the kettle, cuts two slices of homemade bread, and drops them in the toaster. Tension builds in the waiting silence, then eases with the metallic shudder. Saul scrapes on margarine, the kettle whistles and he makes tea, a cup for now and more in the thermos for later. He stirs his tea with a familiar clatter. Jason feels a twinge of memory as wisps of steam rise from the hot spoon which Saul lays carefully in the saucer. He opens the lunchbox, fits the thermos snugly up inside the lid, closes and snaps it shut.

Jason observes all this with pride and senses his father's pride, too, in the simple manly preparations. They sit together in a heavy silence. A grand pronouncement seems hanging in the air. Jason smiles a little to himself when it finally comes.

"Chancey Breen is leaving to drive to North City today," Saul announces. "I asked if he'd take you with him and he said yes. He'll come by at two o'clock. I talked to George on the phone and he said he'll help you find a job up there. Your mother has two hundred dollars to give you. That should do until you find work."

Saul gets up, swallows the last of his tea, tucks his lunchbox under one arm, and walks out of the house.

The Last Half of the Year

Saul Dade was only fourteen when he'd spent his first summer in the lumber camps of central Newfoundland. It was there he'd learned his earliest lessons about what it meant for one of his generation to grow up and be a man. These lessons had mostly to do with the necessity and endurance of hard work but one of a somewhat different kind occurred in the loggers' bunkhouse on a Sunday afternoon. It was their one day to relax — if you could call it that — by reading dime store novels, shaving, washing themselves and their clothes, picking lice off their bodies and squishing them between their fingers, unconsciously searching out the grace notes of kerosene, plus tobacco and wood smoke, that lay beneath the deep repulsive body odour that had been a part of their lives since the day they'd arrived.

Though he'd been obliged to leave school at an early age, Saul Dade remained an ambitious reader and that day he was sitting at a rough-hewn table slowly working his way through the copy of Shakespeare's *Hamlet* that he'd bought out of the twenty dollars his mother had given him for the trip. Mickey Doyle, a boy not much older than Saul himself, had been staring at him for a long time, then suddenly strode across the bunkhouse and slapped the book right out of Saul's hands. Saul winced to see the delicate volume skitter over the rough planked floor. Then Mickey got his foul breath and rotten teeth right up in Saul's face: "What you reading that shit for, Dade? This here is a *bunk*house, not a fucking *school*house."

The loggers looked up from their naps and boredom and Zane Grey paperbacks to see what would happen next.

Saul restrained his impulse to grab Mickey Doyle by the throat. He didn't much like fighting though he would if provoked enough. Instead, allowing himself to be guided by something that he would later think of as pure instinct, he retrieved the book from the floor, opened it, and spoke aloud to the whole room the words he saw when his eyes fell upon the page:

What is a man if his chief good and market of his time / Be but to sleep and feed?

The dramatic question, poetic yet somehow plain-spoken too, brought silence to the room. Saul glanced up to see expectant faces peering out at him from the rows of wooden bunks. He realised with a shock that they were waiting for an answer.

A beast. No more, he proclaimed, and snapped the book shut in Mickey's face.

With murmurings and small approving nods, the men returned to their occupations. One thing was clear: despite their gaunt unshaven faces, their myrrh-encrusted hands, the filthy singlets draped over their bean-fed frames, despite the nagging injuries and mind-numbing drudgery of their work, not a man among them wanted to be considered a beast. And Saul, with his Shakespeare, had somehow suggested that Mickey was being just that.

"Fucking bullshit," Mickey said, sensing he'd been bested, though not sure how, and stomped out, leaving Saul astounded that just two lines from *Hamlet* could be used to such remarkable effect. That day he learned it was by sometimes trusting to the unseen that a man can get himself out of a jam.

Two days later Mickey Doyle disappeared from the camp, the consensus being that he'd either bolted or been eaten by a bear. No one seemed to care much either way. Thereafter the young Saul Dade developed his reputation as a studious labouring man. His fellow loggers left him to his reading and sometimes even displayed a curious pride in his determination to find in books the wisdom they were satisfied to absorb from their work and time on earth. Saul patiently picked the lice from his body and clothes, washed and shaved himself daily, trimmed and combed his hair, and somehow did it all without seeming to judge those who saw it as a losing battle and simply let themselves go for the weeks and months they were in the woods. He bought books in Grand Falls and ordered more from magazines. At home in Birthlayn he bought his own oil and lamp for reading deep into the night so that his father, the cantankerous old Simon, wouldn't bark at him for wasting kerosene.

At nineteen, his studious reputation was enhanced by grey hair that crept first into his temples and then slowly increased until, by the age of twenty-five, he was as silver-haired as any man twice his age.

...

Little Jasie Dade was the kind of boy women would give a nickel to in church for holding their purses while they went to take Communion. Same thing in the smoke-filled bingo hall for fetching them a few more bingo cards. He always got the best marks in the little Birthlayn schoolhouse and when he went to the big school in nearby Princeton he still finished first in his class. He always sat patiently as his mother unwound skein after skein of yarn from his thin tired arms. He always picked his berries clean. He played all sports and games fairly, bravely, and well. Sometimes he fought, but only in matters of honour; he preferred wrestling to fisticuffs, and no matter what, always stopped once he'd bloodied another boy's nose. He fasted three hours before Holy Communion, gave his spare change to the foreign missions, and at home in the evenings he often knelt at his mother's side and said novenas. He did his chores without complaint and his homework faithfully every single night from Grade One to the end of school.

So the question on everyone's lips was, what happened? How on earth, having left home perfectly intact at the age of sixteen to go to university, had the good boy they'd all once known as little Jasie Dade so swiftly come to wrack and ruin?

...

Chancey Breen was supposed to come by at two o'clock but it was much later when he finally did pull up outside the house and blow his horn. No need, since Jason was sitting on the front steps when the blue Ford Fairlane slid into view, its backseat jammed with cardboard boxes and a large mattress wrapped in thick clear plastic across the roof. A yellow nylon rope was looped several times over the mattress, under the roof and across the backseat. This kept the rear doors from opening and the rear windows from closing all the way. It also meant, since there were only the two bucket seats in front, that there would be no hitchhikers, which was fine with

Jason. He also briefly considered the predicament of rain, but shrugged to himself and decided to say nothing as he shouldered his duffle and walked up the gravel bank to the car. For reassurance, he felt one more time for the fold of twenties in the back pocket of his jeans.

Chancey shut off the engine and got out with his keys to unlock the trunk.

"You all set, Jasie?" he said.

Funny how the older guys still called him that.

"'Cause once we puts the pedal to the metal there's no turnin' back. You got that, right?"

"Got it."

Jason climbed in and pulled the door to with a deep thump.

"How's she holdin' up?" he asked, patting the dashboard. It was his usual opening gambit whenever he got into someone's car.

"This piece of shit!" Chancey cocked an eyebrow, then cackled at the joke. "She'll get us where we're going, buddy. Don't you worry."

There was more challenge than reassurance in his tone.

Jason had strong memories of Chancey Breen from his early childhood. He'd always been impressed by the fact that Chancey had up and quit school at fifteen to spray-paint cars for a living. At the softball games in the Groves, Chancey always parked his car of the moment at the bottom of the rocky lane and with his overalls and work boots covered in the paint of the day he would stroll up to the field in his own good time, his personal softball bat slung carelessly over his shoulder. Despite his slight frame Chancey was the only player ever to hit the ball all the way from home plate clear past the meadow and over the trees into the pond.

But the most impressive thing about Chancey was that he only had one lung. That was the story anyway, and it was said that when he exhaled the smoke only came out one nostril. The right one. Jason had never actually seen this marvel and although he had reasoned it out to be anatomically doubtful so many of the older boys had sworn to it that, sitting on the step earlier, Jason had formed a silent resolution to satisfy his curiosity once and for all.

"Hey, you wanna smoke, Chancey?" he said, perhaps a tad too eagerly, and held out a fresh deck of Rothmans.

"Nope."

Disappointed, Jason felt obliged to have one, lit up, and resolved to try again later.

"And we're off like a whore's drawers on payday," chuckled Chancey. Jason saw him toss a quick glance at the empty step before tromping on the gas.

The car lurched toward the High Mountains.

...

Of the many chores Saul Dade performed at his father's behest, making splits was the one he always undertook without reluctance. He never failed to find something gratifying in the smell and feel of dry wood and in the sharp elusive notes it sometimes sang separating under the blade.

"Aim between the knots," his older brother Edmund had told him when Saul was still a boy, and Saul had happily discovered that if he followed this simple advice the thick junks did tend to split cleanly down the middle instead of grabbing axe and arms in a fierce struggle. He became adept and was soon carrying his own armfuls of thin, sweet-smelling splits into the house.

The advice about splits had been Edmund's only lasting gift before leaving Newfoundland. Another of Saul's older brothers had died in the sanatorium in St. John's, a sister had expired years ago from an unnamed disease, and all the rest, like Edmund, moved to Canada or the United States once they'd come of age. The only one who wrote home regularly was his sister Agnes in Boston. In the meantime, he and his younger brother Anthony were left to keep up the house and land and somehow satisfy the necessary illusion that the old man, Simon Dade, was, in his late seventies, still the going concern he'd always been.

Saul would later think that his favourite chore had brought him luck that morning for when he glanced up from the chopping block he saw Willie Breen coming down the Front Pond in his horse and gig. The old bachelor had always assumed the unofficial duty of carrying the news from Princeton, and the job had taken on vital importance since the war. Willie drew near, standing tall in his rig with his coattails flapping, and called out two words in passing:

"Proclamation ... courthouse ..."

Saul dropped his axe immediately and headed for the Harbour Road.

Little Jasie Dade had often sat in that golden patch of morning sunlight thrown across the kitchen table. That's where he'd so often watched his mother work her magic with the flour dust dancing in the sunbeams, whitening her busy hands. He'd heard the rhythmic squeaking of the bread pan as she stood elbow-deep in dough, and the whisper of that dough cut with a sharp blade, revealing yeasty pock marks, then shaped and folded into loaves of ivory smoothness by those same white hands. He'd watched her flatten the dough with a rolling pin and cut it into strips with scissors to make golden crust for pies. He saw layer cakes turned onto cooling racks and held his breath during the slow, perfect peeling away of the waxed paper.

And her bounty at these times was legion: clumps of brown sugar melting in his mouth, icings and sauces licked from mixing spoons and beaters, apple slices tinged with cinnamon, generous apple cores, apple peels that curled like red garlands, dates and candied fruit, fresh bread dripping with salty butter to be licked from his fingers.

A radio sat on a shelf above the fridge with its two heavy brown knobs — one turned it on and off with a loud snap, the other sent a little red stick scuttling across the dial in search of stations — and a gold-threaded speaker cloth through which flowed the music of their lives. *Treat me nice / treat me good / treat me like you always should / I'm not made of wood / And I don't have a wooden heart:* so went one song which, for some reason, Jasie always thought of as being sung by a German toymaker. Then there was Little Jimmy Brown for whom the chapel bells kept ringing and Tom Dooley who had to hang down his head and cry because he'd killed some poor girl on a mountain and Big Bad John who died so bravely in the coal mine, and sixteen tons, and the company store, and the wind they called Mariah. And there was a radio contest where he and his mother would try to solve the riddle of what was inside the Mystery Teapot — when they did manage to solve it their entry didn't get drawn and he never got the thrill of hearing their name on the radio —and the prize money would grow and grow and Jasie longed to win it for his mother and he dreamed up different ways to give it to her if he ever did. His favourite idea was to leave it on the kitchen table as a surprise along with a sad little note explaining that he'd decided to run away from home.

...

Jason knew what Chancey was thinking as the car pulled away from the house: *no one was waving goodbye*. But that was okay. His mother had helped him pack. She'd given him the money and told him to be careful. That was all he needed. He knew she was sitting at the kitchen table right now, right where he'd sat that morning in the oblong patch of sunlight, and he felt her eyes upon him to the last as the big car lumbered up the road and out of sight.

Once beyond Birthlayn the grey road coursed through a long alleyway of spruce trees and occasional bogs, then veered left to follow a sea lane called the Southeast Arm, which was the site of the annual Princeton regatta. Jason recalled the first summer he'd walked in his Sunday suit all the way from Birthlayn to Princeton to see the regatta. It was a dirt road back then, and a disappointing coat of dust had formed on his shiny new shoes. When he got there, already dog tired, he saw men in white shirts asleep on the grass, everywhere the litter of paper bags and tickets stubs, all for the sake of the sleek racing shells he saw far out on the dark waters of the arm. There was thirst, the failed promise of a candied apple, and dying to use the bathroom — a thing he achieved by running as far as he could into an open meadow and, in full view of the milling crowd, just doing it.

The car surged over a rise to reveal the grey expanse of Princeton beach, the white clapboard steeple of the old courthouse still its most prominent landmark. To his left, at the rocky northern tip of the harbour, he saw the dark silhouettes of warehouses, hangars, and Quonset huts on the American naval base where Jason had occasionally gone as a boy to marvel at the flag-festooned battleships, the screaming jet fighters, and fountains of free Coca-Cola.

Chancey skirted past Princeton on the outer beach road and crossed the lift bridge over the gut. It wasn't long then before the houses disappeared and they were speeding along the access road to the highway.

But Jason's thoughts were still back at Princeton beach. He was thinking about his father and how it was said that when Saul Dade was a young man he would go down to the beach even on the worst kind of days, dive into the breakers and swim so far from shore that he would disappear from view. He had no fear of the water, they said. But Jason had seen his father swim only once, on a hot July day like this one. He could picture it now as if it had happened this morning: Saul, standing to his knees in the water wearing a pair of tan-coloured swim trunks, splashing the water onto his arms and stomach, waiting, waiting, waiting, as Jason watched for the moment when his father would take the cold plunge, which he did, at last, by simply letting himself fall backwards onto the sparkling surface and churning his feet like an outboard motor, head and shoulders like a prow cutting the waves with speed and grace for just a very few seconds until he stood up again, but enough time for little Jasie to call out to his mother at the wonder of it (Daddy's swimming! Daddy's swimming!) and when it was over Saul walked to the shore, dried himself with a towel, and left his son forever with that solitary glimpse of the daring young man he'd been, alive in another time.

...

Back in those days the Princeton courthouse, a white clapboard structure of minor stateliness, still stood all to itself at the north end of the Great Beach. It shimmered like a mirage in the heat as Saul Dade made his way toward it over the blanched and corroded stones. When he could finally see the proclamation, like a postage stamp on the dark green door, he barely resisted an undignified scramble over the rocks toward it. But he restrained himself because he thought someone might be watching, perhaps through a window in one of the small square-eyed bungalows that backed the beach along the edge of town. And when at last he stood and read the ornate lettering, he saw that the proclamation fulfilled his every hope and expectation. He was indeed between the ages of 18 and 35, he had a sound physique and good eyesight, he was well over 5 feet 2 inches tall, he was single, and, yes, despite having been pulled out of school at an early age, he had taught himself to read and write very well indeed. The corners of his mouth turned upwards into a tiny smile. Thanks to the war, Saul Dade finally had a future. Without a moment's hesitation he went inside the courthouse and enlisted in His Majesty's Navy.

...

On the Dades' kitchen wall, four ceramic ducks of diminishing size trail after one another in eternal flight toward some unseen horizon. A wooden table painted a soft yellow stands in front of the window. At supper, the scented steam rises from the pots and pans, wafts from the grinning mouths of the teapot and the kettle, and migrates to the table where it wanders up from plates and bowls and cups and saucers. The room is alive with stirring, spreading, pouring, slicing, sipping, passing, lifting, chewing, savouring, smelling.

The food is good. Root crops grown in the garden. Chicken and eggs from the henhouse. Beef from George Breen's slaughterhouse. Trout from Birthlayn's brooks and ponds, cod from the sea, salmon from the rivers, game from the woods and barrens, fruit from the berried marshes. It's all so very good.

Ana's desserts are hot and sweet and sticky and, in a glorious instance of sugary excess, cupfuls of blueberry or partridgeberry or bakeapple jam are scooped out of pots and poured hot over thick slices of blueberry or partridgeberry or bakeapple pie topped yet again by spoonfuls of thick fresh cream.

And tea, hot sweet tea, for everyone except Sarah, who's not old enough yet.

And sometimes Saul will say, "Come here and stir my tea for me, Jasie. That's a good boy." And Jasie will slide down from his seat to perform this cherished task. And sometimes, for mischief's sake, Saul will touch the hot spoon with its wisps of steam off the back of Jasie's hand, and Jasie feels just enough pain and surprise to laugh instead of cry, and the others laugh too at his startled reaction, though his mother can be seen at times to wince with mild concern.

At other times Saul (especially if he's had a few drinks at the Legion in Princeton) will say, "There's lots around here not getting this tonight, you know. Oh, they might have a big car in the driveway, but you mark my words, there's nothing like this on the table. You can write that down in your little black book. Not everything is what it seems around here. Believe half what you see and nothing you hear and you'll learn the rights of that soon enough."

And the youngsters grow quiet in the face of this curious anger. It puzzles them and makes them a little afraid.

"One day you'll understand," he says, annoyed by their silence. "Now finish up and get away. And bless yourselves before you leave the table."

Jason held out the Rothmans pack a second time. This time, Chancey took one and jabbed the cigarette lighter into the Fairlane's magnificent dashboard. Unfortunately though, while driving and smoking he kept himself in profile and Jason couldn't tell if smoke was pouring out the left nostril or no.

He's on to me, Jason thought.

Chancey stubbed the cigarette out into the overflowing ashtray, then released the ashtray with his free hand and somehow also got the driver's side door open to empty it into the road. The tires squealed and Jason got a whiff of burnt rubber as a centrifugal force pinned him to the passenger door.

"Oops!" Chancey laughed, as he clicked the ashtray back in place and took the wheel again in both hands. "Better watch it. Wouldn't wanna ruin my precious cargo."

Precious cargo? The contents of those rackety boxes, maybe. Or something inside that seedy mattress on the roof? Or stashed in the trunk? Drugs? Or was it just a sly dig at his passenger? Possible interpretations flooded Jason's mind as the Fairlane barrelled along the access road. They had the windows down and the radio blasting; the plastic on the mattress overhead flapped madly in the wind. Jason realised it didn't matter what Chancey meant. The important thing was to be once again, for the first time in six long months, moving beyond Princeton and Birthlayn.

"You wanna toke?"

Chancey was holding a joint as thick and long as a carpenter's pencil.

"Hash or grass?"

"Only nature's finest here, Jasie."

Jason pushed in the lighter. When it popped, he bumped the fire-red disc of the lighter against the end of the joint until it caught a spark which he quickly pulled into a bright crackling coal. There was that strong familiar acrid smell. He sucked down and held a generous toke. The weed, he judged, was stalky and not that good.

"No more for me," he said, and handed it to Chancey.

This was no time to be clouding his mind with cheap dope. A crossroads up ahead was fast approaching. When it came into view the sun was already radiating from below the horizon into a pinkish-blue sky marbled with distant clouds. Chancey eased the Fairlane to a stop and they sat there for a while in the throb and fume of the engine staring at the saw-toothed horizon.

Northbound, the Princeton access road ends abruptly — in more of a T than a cross, actually — at the Trans-Canada Highway which runs across the island of Newfoundland west to east from Port aux Basques to St. John's. Today at the crossroads Jason would be turning left for the first time in his life, heading west to Port aux Basques instead of east toward the city. He'd spent many hours last year standing at this same crossroads, the last hitchhiking leg of his weekend trips home from university, darkness and disappointment descending on him as car after car shot by in the vast emptiness of bogs and tangled spruce.

Jason had no idea if The Man was waiting for him in North City and quickly decided it was pointless to worry about that now. There would be enough to deal with once himself and Chancey had made the ferry crossing at Port aux Basques; Jason would be on the mainland then for the first time in his life.

"I say we drive all night and catch a few winks in the morning," Chancey said.

"Sounds good," Jason said.

"Can you drive?" Chancey said.

"No."

"Too bad. I could prob'ly use a break. But, there ya go. Hand us that six-pack on the floor, will ya."

Jason found a six-pack of Dominion by his feet.

"Aw, fuck," said Chancey. "I forgot to bring an opener."

Jason opened the six-pack, pulled out a bottle, and pried the cap off with his teeth.

"I learned that at university," he said.

"Not bad," said Chancey. "Want one?"

"No, thanks."

"Up to yourself. We'll get some more in the morning."

Half an hour later the rolling landscapes of the Avalon lay in darkness beyond the headlights. Jason watched the road for moose. Alder bushes crowded the narrow highway and sometimes, especially on turns, he could only see a few feet ahead. He felt reassured by the thought that, barring the sudden appearance of a moose, a few feet of road ahead was all he really needed to keep going.

A chill came on with the night; Jason shivered and rolled up his window. Just before it shut he heard voices outside on the slipstream, easy conversation and laughter amid tinkling glassware and the ding of a cash register.

A sign ... at last.

The cozy atmosphere of a barroom coming to him from some place a thousand miles away.

...

Saul Dade enjoyed his three weeks of basic training in St. John's though it barely tested his physical conditioning and taught him little beyond how to march sharply in formation. Soon after, having paraded through the muddy streets of the capital and into the bowels of an enamel-grey warship, his contingent sailed out the harbour. Saul adapted quickly to life at sea. He enjoyed the ship's hard narrow passageways, the antiseptic smell of fresh paint, the challenge of small personal spaces; but most of all he enjoyed the sense of being a functioning unit in a greater order, a single link in the chain of command that led from an ordinary seaman like himself all the way up to Winston Churchill and even the King. He aimed to do his small part and do it well. He was older than most and persisted in his quiet ways, often preferring to read in the bunk while the other men smoked and played cards and traded stories about home.

There were still no uniforms upon arrival in London; instead the men were issued Navy-style greatcoats. Saul's was a little too big for him but he felt sophisticated and manly enough in it just the same, his hands buried comfortably in the large pockets as the contingent was led next day on a walking tour of central London. The flow and noise of the great city, the elegance, height and sheer number of buildings so astounded him that as evening fell he was a little embarrassed to notice that his neck was stiff and sore from the day's gawking. The sun's last rays were shining on the Thames by the time they clustered onto Waterloo Bridge across from the Parliament Buildings. In the fading sunlight the impressive edifices, to Saul's eyes at least, took on an aspect of burnished gold. A few months ago he could never have imagined being *here*. How *could* he have imagined making his way in so short a time from tiny insignificant Birthlayn to the very heart of the British Empire? As Big Ben tolled sombrely into the evening, he fought back foolish tears.

No one, not even the old man, could take this moment away from him.

He was assigned to further training in Devonport and it was there, two days later, that he finally got a uniform, along with a hammock and blanket for use on board ship. He tied the hammock to the thick steam pipes overhead so that he was sleeping with his face mere inches from a cast iron ceiling. He had to be wary of sitting up too fast and giving himself a nasty smack on the head. The crossing, he realised, had been the luxury part of the experience. As an ordinary seaman assigned to the merchant marine, life was going to be a lot less glamorous. He had to remind himself that he was here, after all, not on some grand adventure to see the world but to play his own small part in putting the boots to Mr. Hitler.

At first, he found his beribboned sailor's cap, the striped bib and bell-bottomed trousers, a little at odds with a military bearing, but he wore it with pride once he noticed the respect it garnered in the streets of the port city. Despite that, however, and the special events that were arranged for himself and his mates in London, Saul decided to use his first four-day leave to go to Scotland instead. He knew several men from home who were enlisted in the Forestry Service there, encamped outside a little town called Ballater. It would be great to visit them, he thought, so that after the war they could all reminisce about the time they'd been together in a place so far away from Birthlayn.

...

The 'lectricity was always going out in Birthlayn when Jasie Dade was little. When it did, his mother would light the lamps and show him and his brother Georgie how to use their hands to make dog and rabbit shadows on the wall. Sometimes they played string games, other times she'd have Jasie hold a skein or two of sweet-smelling yarn which she'd ravel into a ball. But most times, Jasie would sit beside the oil lamp and crack open one of the books from the encyclopedia that their Aunt Agnes had been sending them from the United States. Every few weeks a new one would arrive encased in the stiff cardboard which they peeled back to reveal yet another shiny volume moving them a little further along the alphabetic road from Aardvark to Zephyr. Saul Dade took a secret pride in watching Jasie lose himself again and again in those books, and was proud of his sister too for caring enough to buy the books and send them home.

One time when the lights went out and the lamps were lit, Jasie sat in the rocking chair with his father's pipe in his mouth and his mother's knitting needles in his hands and started rocking and they all had a grand laugh at seeing him imitate both parents in one go like that.

And then there was the time at the school concert when his mother dressed him up in a Guernsey sweater, rubber boots, and an old salt n' pepper cap, and with that same pipe in hand he gave a recitation that the teacher, Miss Crockwell, had found for him in the newspaper. The crowded schoolroom that night had a little stage set up in one end, and when the curtain opened on the lone boy there was nervous laughter at first, but then a sudden hush as he took the pipe from his mouth, and began:

> The typical Newfoundlander,
> And I'm proud that I am one,
> Besides the King's good English
> Has a language all his own.
> For instance, if you meet one
> And enquire about his health,
> He's not "just fine" nor "like the bird"
> He's "first rate boy - How's yourself?"

And on and on he went through the long recitation not missing a beat until he finished with a small bow to a burst of applause.

His parents always enjoyed going to the schoolhouse to get his report cards and hearing what the teacher had to say about him. Georgie was devil-may-care, but did well enough at school, though he quickly became more interested in hunting birds and snaring rabbits. Sarah also did well once she started, but it was clear from the beginning that little Jasie was going to be the one to watch.

Jason and Chancey woke up the next day, grumpy and sleep-deprived, in the parking lot of a motel. After driving all night as planned, Chancey had pulled into the parking lot at sunrise and they'd slept in the car. Now, after baking in the heat for several hours, Jason found himself sweaty and clammy and thirsty beyond belief. Chancey drove in grim silence to a gas station, but perked up after an apple flip and chocolate milk. He bought a fresh six-pack, and they were on the road again.

When they got back to open highway, Jason rolled down the window and let the wind once again caress his face. The landscape was different, he noticed, here on the west coast of the island: majestic stands of birch instead of pervasive evergreens, and *real* mountains, soft and blue in the distance, like the ones you'd see in a photograph. And for a time they drove beside the widest, wildest river — there was no way you could call it a *brook* — that he'd ever seen.

Freedom would be rafting down that river like Huckleberry Finn, wrapping yourself around those mountains and disappearing into that sky...

"This isn't going to work," Chancey said.

"Hmm?"

"The ferry doesn't leave until almost noon tomorrow and I don't want to spend another night sleeping in the car."

"So what do we do?"

"Go into Stephenville and get a motel for the night. Get up early and make the ferry."

"Okay."

"Good. That's settled."

Chancey sighed and relaxed into the seat, a beer bottle tucked between his thighs, streams of cigarette smoke plunging from the one visible nostril. The stench of stale tobacco and last night's skunk weed hung heavily in the air.

Chancey's bright blue eyes and broken front tooth, the careless shock of blond hair that kept falling across his nose, reminded Jason of a cartoon canine in some old Walt Disney classic. He remembered a Saturday morning the previous July, a month after he'd finished high school and several weeks before the start of his abortive university year, when he'd noticed something unusual about the coloured comics in the weekend newspaper. That morning the comics had come alive in a way they'd never done before. They hadn't moved or spoken to him or anything crazy like that, but they'd definitely become something more than just cartoon figures on a page. He'd discovered a deeper meaning in the whimsical faces and simple declarations ballooned above their heads. There was a sly wink to him now, an invitation of sorts, that hadn't been there before, a shared insight into things that was always clever, humorous and wise. When he went on to university that fall he'd found the new awareness spreading to famous faces on album covers. Eerie looks from black light posters and glamorous glances from magazines also shared with him these secret knowing smiles.

That July morning about a year ago had been the start, the first real sign, that things in his life were going to change in ways he could never imagine.

It took longer than expected for the road sign that said Stephenville to finally appear. Meanwhile, Jason watched Chancey struggle to keep his eyes open. Once, he actually dozed off at the wheel, only to be startled awake by the abrupt noise of tires on gravel when the car drifted onto the shoulder.

"You have to start talking to me, Jasie, or I'm gonna fuckin' nod off here! I had a hard enough time staying awake last night with you just sitting there. You're supposed to *talk* to help keep me awake. That's your *job*!"

"Cigarette?"

"Fuck the cigarettes! Talk!"

So Jason talked. He started with the first thing his eyes fell on — Chancey's foot on the accelerator. This led to a short reflection on energy and drive and the importance of movement in the world ... *of actually getting somewhere.* He spoke, more wistfully, of disappearing into the sky above the blue-topped mountain in the distance. He observed how the white billowy clouds looked like giant summer sheep and this triggered recollections of Chancey's glories at softball, homerun after homerun, silver paint on his steel-toed boots as he rounded the bases time and again, forcing all hands into the woods below the field to search for the ball ... *dear St. Anthony, dear St. Anthony, come around ...* which, in turn, inspired memories of late summer hayrides in Birthlayn meadows and then, feeling the pressure to keep going no matter what, Jason talked about time; the past, the present, and the future, he said, were all the same thing. It was something he'd read at university last year, though he still wasn't sure what it meant, but he figured it had something to do with the sun being the source of all life on earth, setting up the days and nights and weeks and months of the year and how the road ... *the road goes on forever ... the wheels on the bus go round and round ... and the wheels on this thing could fall off and burn and we'd still be somewhere ... in time ... and wherever that is, it has to come from and lead to somewhere else in time, and that means ...*"

"SHUT THE FUCK UP!"

"...!"

"Jesus Christ, Jasie. What the fuck was that all about? Look, b'y, just chew off another one of those beer caps for me, will ya, and roll up another joint. That'll have to keep me awake because I don't want to hear another goddamn word out of you. I got half a mind to put you out on the goddamn highway right now."

Jason bit off the bottle cap as another large road sign loomed.

"Can you read what's on that sign?"

Jason read aloud: STEPHENVILLE ←12 MILES
STEPHENVILLE CROSSING → 5 MILES

"Well?" Chancey said, "what do you think? Stephenville or Stephenville Crossing?"

"I don't know," said Jason.

"Well, I'm fucked if *I* know," Chancey said. "I s'pose they got hotels in either place, do they? Which way do you *think* we should go?"

"Whichever way you want to go is fine with me."

"Fuck, b'y!" Chancey said. "That's not an answer. Make a decision for once in your life, will ya!" He tromped on the gas pedal and Jason felt the Fairlane surge like a wave. "Here, luh, I'll fuckin' help ya make a decision. Okay? Whaddaya say? Left or right? You call it." The big green road sign stood straight ahead on two white wooden pillars set into the gravel shoulder. The road to Stephenville or Stephenville Crossing ran left and right in front of it. Beyond the sign Jason saw a deep ditch, and beyond that, the rough barren of boulders, moss, and tuckamore that they were barrelling straight toward.

"Left or right?" Chancey insisted.

In the fading light Jason watched as Chancey's cartoon character took on the sinister aspect of a speed demon, but, still, Jason held his peace and Chancey kept the pedal to the metal.

Finally recognizing the futility of his little Mexican standoff, Chancey said Fuck it, let up on the accelerator, and dramatically wrenched the steering wheel to the right. Normally, he'd have made it, but he didn't factor in the bloody mattress. On the sharp turn it caught and held enough of the updraft to give the Fairlane the added heave and lift it needed to achieve momentary flight. First two, then four of its tires left the road. The car turned onto its side in a grinding rush of sparks, then flipped over onto the roof, shredding mattress stuffing all over the road before it disappeared into the ditch.

...

One July day at a field hockey game in the Groves, little Jasie Dade played spectacularly in goal, making save after unbelievable save until his team was ahead five to nothing. Then he suddenly announced that he wanted to switch sides. Everyone laughed and shook their heads and said, "Sure, b'y, go ahead." Of course,

Jasie played even more spectacularly for the losing team as they slowly fought back to tie the game. They lost in the end, 6 - 5, but it was such a magnificent loss that it actually felt like a victory.

Thanks to Jasie, everyone went home that day feeling like a winner.

Little Jasie Dade is a lover of the long shot. He will go so far as to deliberately stack the odds against himself in order to heighten the thrill of coming up a winner. He loves to fall far behind in a footrace, for example, then catch up and catch up and catch up until right at the end he crosses the finish line first.

Sometimes, his imagination runs wild dreaming of longer and more adventuresome long shots, bigger and more spectacular comebacks with more and more momentous things riding on them: down three games to none in the NHL finals and still winning the Stanley Cup; some bottom-of-the-ninth-bases-loaded-two-men-out-full-count-grand-slam win of the World Series; or, more fancifully, some extraordinary comeback that saves his little sister from kidnappers, or the Earth from alien invaders.

He wonders what it would be like to someday take the longest long shot ever taken in the entire history of the world.

August

August in Birthlayn was all about making hay. Youngsters were forbidden to roam in certain meadows during the spring and summer months to allow the grass to grow straight and tall and be easily felled with scythes. Saul Dade never owned cattle or sheep or horses so Jasie and his brother Georgie would go to other people's meadows to help with making the hay. There was nothing for the youngsters to do at first except stand around and watch, for clearly, mowing hay was strictly men's work.

Little Jasie knew from experience how hard it was to wield a scythe. There was one, hanging from a beam under the house, that he'd never seen his father use. Once, when his father was away working up north Jasie took down the scythe and snuck into the meadow with it. He discovered how unwieldy a thing it actually was — it seemed to wrestle with his arms — and no matter how hard he tried to force the long curving blade to behave itself and cut the grass, the pointed tip, again and again, wound up stuck into the sod. This little adventure gave him a real appreciation of the skill that Birthlayn men displayed all day long in the hot meadows, swinging their scythes over and over with seemingly nothing more than a simple turn at the waist, causing the tall grass to collapse into orderly swaths at their feet.

When the men took a break, beer that had been cooling in the brook would be brought and the brown stubby bottles raised to their sweating faces. They drank deeply and the golden ale would look and smell to the lurking youngsters like the most refreshing thing on earth, and if one of them gave little Jasie a sip there was nothing in that sour yeasty taste that made the boy alter his opinion in the slightest. Jasie often wished that the brook behind his house flowed with beer instead of water and that he could throw himself down onto the grassy bank whenever he wanted and suck back the elixir in great gulps, the way he saw horses and cows suck thirstily from the brook on hot summer days.

The youngsters could at last be helpful when the time came to make the hay. They took to the meadows with their specially-made short-handled pitchforks, shook the hay from the cocks and windrows onto the open ground, and turned it every few hours from its dry side to its green side, this for a few hopefully sunny days, until it cured.

When it was time to stow the hay the youngsters came into their full usefulness. First, they would carefully arrange and stow the hay aboard the truck and then, after it was delivered, inside the bulk and loft of the stable. It was an important job, especially the first part, for if the hay was poorly stowed on the truck, part of the load could slip off in transit with disastrous results for the youngsters who, as a reward for their labours, always rode on top. Once, in Jasie's time, a load had slipped off and in the tumbling melee one of his cousins accidently got a pitchfork in the guts.

So Jasie and Georgie and the other youngsters took the job very seriously.

It was because of this work that little Jasie came to regard it the perfect image of manliness to mow hay all day long in a hot summer meadow and he longed for the day when *he* could swing a scythe in a sweat-stained singlet and wipe his brow with a spotted handkerchief. So, he was delighted when his father came home from working up north that time and took it into his head to mow the tall grass beside the house. Jasie had always wondered if his father really did know how to use the scythe. He looked on with enormous anticipation as Saul Dade confidently took the scythe from under the house, smartly stroked the long curved blade with the whetstone, and then, as his boy swelled with secret pride, effortlessly mowed the tall grass with incredible gentleness and grace, laying it in perfectly arrayed swaths upon the ground.

...

Once Saul Dade had conquered the anxiety of busy London streets and a crowded train station, he found himself feeling cautiously self-assured in his comfortable railway car as the English countryside drifted past. The hillsides of his youth, he realised, meandered somewhat like those outside, though not nearly so far nor so freely before being hemmed in by dense spruce forest. In fact, the hills sliding by the train window were more reminiscent of Paddy's Cove, the place further down the shore from Birthlayn where he'd spent so many summers as a boy shipping to his Uncle Mike. Saul remembered how he'd achieved a certain notoriety during those summers because of his fearlessness in diving headlong into the white-foamed breakers off Paddy's Cove beach. He'd learned that a submerged swimmer can avoid the treacherous heave and pull of the breakers by keeping an eye on the surface and calmly waiting for the foam and frothy bubbles to clear. Once past the breakers, he would stroke so strongly through the buoyant water that he often had the whimsical idea that he could, if he wanted, pull himself up onto the pale green surface and walk across it like Jesus did in the Bible.

But all this, he knew, was pretty much lost on the Birthlayn buddies who were waiting for him in Ballater. They hadn't spent their summers in Paddy's Cove and, as the years went by, they'd made little comment, and even appeared a little jealous, as Saul's swimming prowess somehow passed into the stuff of local legend.

Upon arrival, Ballater had an almost magical effect on Saul Dade. It seemed to him a *perfect* small town. He particularly loved the little stone church which itself stood on the site of an ancient monastery. Back home, such dignified antiquities, such ancient orderly towns didn't exist. In fact, he'd never heard Birthlayn referred to as a *town*, and certainly not a *community*; it was simply a *place*, as if defined by location alone and not by its past or people. He learned from the talkative porter on the train that Ballater had fewer inhabitants than Birthlayn, yet it had this beautiful stone church, an all-grade school, a number of charming public buildings, attractive streets and houses, and even a cosy pub called The Thunder Stone where Saul imagined he and the boys from home would gather for pints that same evening.

But, sitting at the pub later on, Saul worried that things hadn't gone so well with the boys at the lumber camp that morning. His concerns seemed justified when he saw Benjamin Breen enter the pub alone. He and Ben were first cousins, their mothers being sisters who'd come up the shore from Paddy's Cove to marry Birthlayn men, but the two families had never really been close. In truth, Saul had always felt a little removed from fellows his own age in Birthlayn, perhaps because of the many summers he'd spent in Paddy's Cove, but the exciting idea of everyone meeting up in foreign parts had wiped any such reservations from his mind.

"Where are the others?" he asked, once Ben was seated with a pint.

Ben took a long careful sip, took tobacco fixings out of his pocket and started rolling a cigarette. His hair was wet and neatly combed and he smelled of aftershave.

"Help yourself, Saul," he said, placing tobacco and rolling papers on the table.

"No. Thank you."

Saul was never much of a smoker — he was fond of saying that a pack could last him a month — and he'd dropped smoking altogether since joining up. Tobacco's cravings and paraphernalia, he figured, would be a nuisance on board ship.

"Are the others coming?" he persisted, already piecing together the reason he and Ben would be drinking alone.

"They're all done in after work, Saul. Still not used to the long days."

That was a lie. When had these men *not* worked long days?

Oh, there'd been some initial excitement when Saul turned up in the logging camp that morning. The fellows were happy enough to see someone from home. But things took a turn when one of the Scotsman showed up with a camera and suggested they pose for a photograph. Then someone else found a rifle. Saul was immediately uncomfortable with the idea of striking some sort of warlike pose holding a rifle. It seemed foolish — a rifle was not even part of his onboard equipment — and the whole procedure reminded him of one of those photo shops where people dress up like characters in a dime-store novel. It was unseemly behaviour for men at war and Saul found it difficult to hide his unease. He went along with the charade as best he could and, with a sheepish grin, even agreed to have his picture taken.

But his discomfort was obvious and it was quickly taken by the others as disdain. He'd observed a kind of silent invective pass through their eyes, from one to the other, an unspoken tirade that, as he later imagined it, went something like this: So *you're* the big fighting man come here to lord it over us in your *uniform* and show us that we're not *real* fighting men like you; we're only fucking woodcutters and you, *you're* the only one of us who might actually be *killed* in this war, so fuck you then, because we are doing our part the way we see fit and we don't give a *shit* what you think ... and so vanished Saul's hopes for a jolly evening at the pub with his mates, making the stuff of memories for the days after the war.

What was worse, Saul was beginning to see that maybe he *had* come to Ballater to lord it over the boys. After all, he hadn't been obliged to wear his naval uniform. And he didn't have to pose for the photograph with that look on his face that had so clearly shown his disdain. Ben struck a match and Saul raised his glass.

"Cheers," they said, and the glasses clinked.

Saul had already resolved to make a quick return to London and salvage what was left of his leave.

...

The "hotel" Chancey found in Stephenville turned out to be little more than a room above a roadside bar. It had dirty red industrial carpet, wood-panelled walls, stained ceiling tiles, a shop-worn dresser, and two single beds tightly made up with what at least looked like clean white sheets. Jason had a nasty scratch on his back, probably from one of the cardboard boxes that had pinned him to the dash, but otherwise he was okay. Chancey had apparently escaped without even a scratch.

Jason soon lost track of the days that followed as he and Chancey spent their mornings and evenings watching the only available channel on a grainy black and white TV. At around noon they would go to the downstairs bar for a feed of fish and chips. Chancey would then go see about the car repairs and return towards evening with take-out food for them both.

"I'll pay for the car repairs and this bit of food," he said, "but we'll split the cost of the room. Okay?"

Jason nodded, but he didn't like it. He hadn't planned on spending an extra week, or however long it was, in Stephenville. As the days dragged on he realised that even half the room cost was going to take a serious bite out of his finances. It seemed unfair since he hadn't caused the accident and since, he suspected, Chancey was making a little extra money for himself selling dope in the downstairs bar. This might explain why Chancey strongly suggested Jason avoid hanging around down there after their daily fish and chips at lunchtime. But one day Jason finished his lunch and couldn't face going back to the room, so he said to hell with it, walked up to the bar and ordered himself a beer.

The barroom was large and well-lit, one of those roadside places that packed them in on weekends but didn't do much business otherwise. The beer came ice-cold and well-poured and he sucked it back. The bartender, a small tidy fellow with a nose full of gin blossoms, seemed nice enough. Maybe the place wasn't so bad after all. A fellow with hair like Elvis Presley, and a couple of nice-looking girls, a blonde and a brunette, were in the far end playing pool. Another guy, tall and lanky, came in and joined them.

After the first game ended, Elvis approached and asked the bartender for quarters. Jason could smell the Brylcreem in his hair.

"Just passing through?" he said to Jason.

"We had a car accident outside town. My buddy's gone to see about the damage."

"Yeah, I've seen you come and go. What's your name?"

"Jason Dade. Yours?"

"Elvis. Elvis Murphy," he said, and stuck out his hand.

Jason smiled and accepted the handshake.

"You should come and sit with us, man. Play a little pool."

"Sure."

Jason grabbed his beer and slid down off the bar stool.

...

Little Jasie was going to the store for his mother that day, strolling down the road with a scribbled note and a two-dollar bill in his pocket, when the big dump truck ground to a halt in front of him and a wide passenger door swung slowly open to block the endless view of meadows, pond and sea that lay before him. When he came up alongside he saw a handsome fellow in a white T-shirt and blue jeans sitting behind the wheel, smiling at him with a full set of bright white teeth.

"You need a lift?" the fellow called over the rumble of the engine.

"Sure," Jasie lied. The store was really no distance away, just another couple of minutes on foot and he'd be there, but Jasie didn't want to appear ungrateful — the fellow had taken the trouble to stop, after all — so he climbed up into the cab. As the man leaned across to pull the big door shut, Jasie caught a whiff of Brylcreem amidst the gas fumes and dusty leather. The long metal wand of the gearshift was topped by a hard shiny knob, like a pool ball with the numbers worn off, and the man gripped it deftly and began pushing and pulling his way through the gears as the big truck lumbered on down the road.

Jasie found his feet couldn't touch the floor. It felt grand to be sitting up so high looking out over Birthlayn, like being up in a tree only better since the truck was moving, and this gave an impression of the landscape outside moving too, like on a television screen. He could see the full course of Mrs. Mary's Brook snaking through her meadow, then James's Brook in the next meadow disappearing into the trees. In the large side mirror, he caught a glimpse of his own house where his mother was waiting on her brown sugar and butter and baking powder and whatever else was on the note that suddenly felt like it was burning a hole in his pocket. Then the truck dipped down the Big Hill and the mirror filled with sky as his house dropped out of sight.

"So, where you off to?" the fellow asked.

They had already passed the store.

"To the store," Jasie said, a little web of lies suddenly forming in his head.

It had seemed foolish to get out so soon after having gotten in, so he'd said nothing as the store slipped past and now he was trying to adjust his story so he could get out down by the pond instead, which seemed a respectable distance to ride, but the trouble was there were only a few houses down the pond and not one had a Coca-Cola sign outside to make it look like a store.

"Can you drive?" the fellow said. He shifted into low gear and braked to make the truck whine reluctantly down the steep hill.

"No," said Jasie, thinking it an odd question. Everyone knew children didn't drive. He remembered, though, that sometimes, George Breen would let his boys sit in his lap and steer home from Sunday Mass in Princeton. Is that what the fellow wanted Jasie to do? It did look like fun, all right; Jasie's father would never allow it in their car.

But Jasie was at an end. He couldn't think of another word to say. They were already at the bottom of the hill and the truck had turned left at the bridge and now they were heading up the pond to where the houses grew even more scattered and it must have been obvious to the stranger that there was no store and Jasie was feeling terribly embarrassed to be caught in such a silly lie and in another minute they'd be around the point and on the way down the shore to where there were no houses at all for miles and though his embarrassment inclined him to silence he was increasingly uncomfortable at finding himself so quickly farther and farther from home and he was worried about his mother and her cake, how she was expecting him, and how she'd promised him a nickel for going to the store, and somewhere deep inside himself he found the courage to speak and he said, more firmly than he'd intended, "I'll get out right here."

The man behind the wheel seemed to deliberate a long second or two, then pulled over to the side of the road. He reached across again and threw open the passenger door.

"S' long," he said.

Still incapable of anything but to continue the pretence, Jasie said thanks for the lift and slipped from his seat to the road. He flung the big door shut with both hands and felt curiously relieved as the truck pulled away. Then, annoyed at himself, he immediately ran all the way back to the store and then to the house where his mother, thankfully, after asking what took him so long, a question he shrugged at, still gave him the precious nickel. He scooted back down the road with the nickel pressed hotly in his hand and spent it right away.

...

Saul quickly drained his pint and laid the empty glass on the table. His trip to Ballater had come to naught but he had to be careful not to show his disappointment.

"Thanks for coming, Ben," he said. "It's too bad the other fellows weren't up to it. I'm feeling a little done in myself and I have an early train, so ..."

"Thanks for coming all this way, Saul," Ben replied, and drained his own glass. "Please God we'll all see each other at home soon enough."

Saul knew that was as close as they would ever get to discussing the truth of the situation, and he was about to call it a night when the pub door opened and a most curious-looking man stepped into the bar. Saul watched in some amazement as the heavyset figure strode across the room, handed his walking stick and cloth cap to the barman, and ordered a pint. The amazing thing was that his large bald head seemed, at least in the dim glow of the bar candles, to be covered in tattoos. After a first deep draught the fellow turned to face the room and Saul could plainly see that a swirl of tattoos did indeed cover not only the man's head, but his face and throat as well. Almost against his will, Saul imagined the man's shoulders, chest, and back — he dared descend no further! — also covered in the intricate and colourful designs. And as odd as *that* was, what seemed more peculiar was the fact that everyone quickly went back to chatting and drinking and paid the carnival freak at the bar not the slightest bit of attention. Then, something odder still: the tattooed man looked straight into Saul's eyes and raised his glass as if toasting an old friend. To top it all off, he headed straight toward their table.

Benjamin Breen saw all this too and stared wide-eyed at Saul who returned a small shrug of helplessness.

"Good evening, gentlemen," the stranger said. "Mind if I take a seat?"

The accent was definitely Scottish, but nuanced with something that Saul couldn't quite put his finger on. He was also struggling with the improbable notion that he'd met the fellow somewhere before. Perhaps in a dream?

"Have a seat, yes." Ben, suddenly animated, grandly waved his hand. "Sure, there's plenty of room and we were about to order a couple of pints."

"Two more here," the fellow called loudly without even a backward glance, and, sure enough, in a moment the barkeep came running with two freshly drawn glasses.

"So where are you lads from?" he asked. Saul caught an unsettling glimpse of a mouth full of mostly gold teeth.

"From Newfoundland," Saul answered, then added, " ... across the pond ... " hoping the phrase would add a touch of worldliness.

"Ah, I know it well, though I've never been," the fellow said, pulled a small cloth bag by the drawstring from his front coat pocket, and set about rolling a cigarette. The tattoos ran along the backs of his hands and disappeared up his coat sleeves, even the fingertips had been minutely attended to.

"Smoke?"

Saul thought it might be rude to refuse so he simply said thank you as he was handed the expertly rolled cigarette. Ben was already smoking so the fellow quickly rolled another for himself.

"Turkish," he said with a wink. "The finest smoke there is."

And indeed there was an acrid odour and taste to the tobacco, quite unlike anything Saul had ever smoked before. He sat back in his chair and relaxed. Perhaps the evening might not be such a disappointment after all.

...

Jason Dade had never seen a switchblade, but the one balanced on the bathroom urinal was everything he'd imagined one to be. He was staring at it, trying to make sense of what Elvis Murphy was saying ... he was asking about Jason talking to Elvis's girlfriend at the table. Jason *had* spoken to her, yes, but only in the most ordinary way, chatting with her casually when Elvis went to the bar to get more quarters for the pool table. He hadn't offended her, he didn't think, hadn't said anything impolite or out of the way. Maybe Elvis thought Jason was trying to put the makes on her. Maybe that's why Elvis had left the table and why the other fellow, the tall lanky one, had told Jason to go into the bathroom because Elvis wanted to talk to him. And maybe that's why, in the bathroom, Elvis had lifted his shirt to show Jason the knife tucked under his belt.

"What were you sayin' to my girlfriend out there?" he asked.

"Nuthin'. I wasn't saying nuthin' to your girlfriend."

Elvis held the knife up in front of Jason's face and pressed a button, there was a snap and flash of silver, and that's when Jason realised it was a switchblade. The air was laced with chlorine and piss and the faint sickening smell of Brylcreem. The pipes whistled faintly in the walls, and Jason's heart pounded in his throat.

Elvis balanced the knife on the urinal, stepped back and faced Jason in a gunslinger stance. "I count to three," he said, "and we go for it."

"Not me," said Jason. "No way. You can do whatever you like, but I'm not touching that fucking knife."

The slap in the face left him watery-eyed and stunned.

"I don't care," he continued, "you can kill me if you like. I'm not touching that knife."

Elvis seemed to assess the situation. He picked up the knife, closed it, and put it in his pocket. Then, he clipped Jason on the chin with a roundhouse punch. Jason fell backwards into a cubicle and curled into a ball; Elvis forced his way in and started kicking him in the back. It was a cramped space, so it didn't hurt much, but Jason screamed at the top of his lungs anyway hoping to alert someone outside as to what was happening in the bathroom. The screaming and the absence of any actual physical pain made Jason feel curiously safe and distant from the predicament he was in. He was just getting tired of screaming when Elvis suddenly disappeared. The cubicle door swung carelessly on its hinges for a time. Then, the lanky fellow came in and told Jason it was okay to come out.

Elvis had left the building.

...

One August day in Birthlayn a group of boys were batting fly balls in the meadow behind the schoolhouse. They were catching them for points — ten each, up to a hundred to be the winner — and everything was going along fine until Jasie Dade stole the winning catch right out of Johnnie Breen's glove. Johnnie protested, but Jasie reminded him he hadn't called it.

"I don't give a shit," Johnnie insisted, "I was *under* it."

The others knew Jasie was right, and that Johnnie would never admit it, so they gradually drifted away and left the two boys to sort it out for themselves.

Once they were alone it wasn't long before Johnnie muttered the fighting words that Jasie dreaded to hear: *traitor bastard.*

Jasie hadn't heard the vile expression, a deliberate insult to his mother's ancestry, in a while. He sighed. It was almost six-thirty and he had hoped to get home in time to watch *Leave It to Beaver*. In fact, if it hadn't been for his favourite program coming on, he would have let Johnnie make the catch (though he *hadn't* called it) just to keep the game going. Now though, since he and Johnnie were pretty evenly matched as combatants, it was going to take some time to get him to take those vile words back.

The insult stemmed from the fact that Jasie's mother, Ana Cruet, was born in Princeton, and Princeton, as everyone knew, had at one time been colonised by the French. The Irish arrived soon after the French had been expelled and quickly seized the high moral ground by labelling the French remnant — those who'd stayed and sworn an oath of allegiance to the British Crown — not only as traitors, but also the bearers of questionable offspring to the conquering Brits.

Even though all this was lost upon the Birthlayn youngsters of Jasie's day, the term *traitor bastard* had itself lived on, somehow retaining its harsh currency for an astonishingly long time.

So, to get things going Jasie landed a quick slap — he found it impossible to hit a face with his fist — that reddened Johnnie's cheek and watered his eyes. Johnnie countered with a flurry of poorly aimed blows before Jasie got him around the midsection and threw him hard to the ground.

"Take it back?"

"Go fuck yourself."

The Breen boys were notoriously profane.

The two ten-year-olds carried on their prolonged wrestling match, with the odd body punch thrown in, for over an hour. Then darkness crept out of the trees and Johnnie's mother's voice drifted up to them from their house beside the pond.

"JOHNNIEEEEEEEEEEEE."

"I got to go home," the boy said, flat on his back, Jasie's legs in a scissor-hold around his middle.

"Not 'til you takes it back."

"JOHNNIEEEEEEEEEEEEEEE!!!!!"

"Fuck," said Johnnie, "I takes it back," and Jasie released him from the leg lock.

Johnnie jumped to his feet and cantered down the meadow like a foal.

As it turned out, that fight behind the schoolhouse was the last of its kind that Jasie would have to endure, for by the time he was ten years old something remarkable was happening in Birthlayn. The most recent crop of Birthlayn youngsters had somehow developed loyalties toward one another instead of, as in the past, continuing to spread the sometimes harmful gospel of their parents' heated talk at home. The ridiculous prejudice of the *traitor bastard* was beginning to disappear. Jasie's baby sister, Sarah, who was still in the cradle, would be spared completely.

As Johnnie Breen disappeared into the fading light, Jasie picked up his softball glove and walked home, satisfied that he'd once again, though unknowingly for the last time, defended the family name against dishonour.

...

Saul Dade would never quite recall the sequence of events that night in the Scottish pub: how and when the introductions took place, what got said and by whom, how they got from one topic to another or even what those topics were.

The tattooed man, as it turned out, was a Russian Jew named Petro.

Afterwards, all Saul knew for sure was that he and Petro did most of the talking — Ben looking happily on

— about what must have amounted to a great many things as the night wore on in the smoky haze and din of the crowded room.

They also drank numerous pints of ale.

But Saul would always remember exactly how the night had ended. One by one the patrons had gone home; even the barman said goodnight in the end and left the three of them at their table in the corner. Petro, it also turned out, was the owner of the pub, and once the place had emptied he went behind the bar and pulled three more pints himself. By the time he placed them on the table, however, Benjamin Breen had folded his arms across his chest and nodded off to sleep. Saul, close to falling into his own stupor, was wishing Petro had decided to call it a night instead, but not wanting to appear ungrateful, he willed his hand to grasp the pint and brought it carefully to his lips.

"So, Petro, you're ... you're a Jew?" "Jew" was a very stark word to Saul Dade and he was a little afraid of it. He wasn't even sure if Jews liked to be called Jews. Maybe "of the Jewish faith" or "one of the Chosen people" was more proper?

"That's right," said Petro. "My ancestors were gypsies, as you may have guessed" — he splayed his tattooed fingers — "who wandered in the Ukraine for centuries before they settled near St. Petersburg."

"What brought you to Scotland?"

"My father left Russia before the first war to escape the communists and the pogroms. They were in a race to see who could kill us first and take our money."

Sometime earlier Saul had gradually started hearing the Russian inside Petro's Scottish accent, and the impression had grown on him until, now, the Russian accent was all he could hear.

"But my father managed to get us out with our bit of treasure," Petro continued. "He came here, bought this place and made a good living for us all until he died. My brother and sister returned to the Ukraine. Me, I like it here."

"So this is all yours then?" Saul gestured with his pint to the smoke-filled room.

"Yes! Imagine a man like me with a Scottish pub. It is almost comical."

"I must admit I was a little surprised by the ...," Saul made little circles in front of his own face.

"Only a little?" Petro laughed. "For a few years now I have let someone else manage this place. This gives me time to travel and to explore the things that interest me."

"But why the ...?" Again, the circles.

"The Ukraine is renowned for the art of tattooing. I have made many visits to the land of my ancestors over the years and every time I go there I get a new one." He laughed again and pointed at his own face. "You see I am running out of places to put them."

Saul Dade was keenly aware that he was in the land of his own ancestors, or at least back in Devonport he was close to the birthplace of the one ancestor who'd made the biggest impression on him. Saul had always quietly revered his paternal grandfather, William Dade, a Devonian farmer and fisherman who'd gone soldiering to Newfoundland in the nineteenth century and who'd eventually deserted the army in St. John's to run off and start the Dade family line in Birthlayn. Saul saw no shame in the desertion since hostilities had long since ended and he could appreciate the allurements of land and opportunity that rural Newfoundland must have held. Since virtually everyone else in Birthlayn was of Irish descent, this English ancestor had always set Saul apart in a way of which he was rather fond, even proud. But, as much as he would have loved to exploit the present opportunity to dig into his English past, he couldn't, for his grandfather was, in reality, little more than a memory, and that only of a scratched and faded tintype that had lain around the house when he was a boy. His father, Simon, strangely shared none of his son's enthusiasm for ancestry and by the time Saul was old enough to begin asking serious questions about the heavily-bearded figure on the tintype it had simply disappeared, most likely thrown away. It angered Saul that his father could have so callously discarded this treasure of the past.

Things weren't any better on his mother's Irish side where the trail of ancestors dried up after just a couple of generations.

As the years passed, Saul's romantic longings for his roots persisted. Even if he would never have a life outside Birthlayn he could at least entertain some sense of a life *before* Birthlayn, an idealized view of an Old World that still ran in his blood.

In the end, the gravestone that his paternal grandparents, William and Clara Dade, shared on Dixon's Hill in Princeton remained Saul's only tangible connection to that Old World of his ancestors, though it remained a story in stone, largely untold. This perhaps explained the sudden thrust of envy he felt toward

Petro, the man with the marks of his ancestors inscribed upon his face.

"So where did your people settle when they stopped being gypsies?" Saul asked, his head growing heavy, his tongue ever more thick.

"Lakhta, near Petersburg. It's not a town really, more just a place."

Like Birthlayn, Saul thought.

"Why there?" he asked.

"Ah, the event that changed the course of my family's history! You see, my great-great-great-grandfather — Saul jealously registered each *great* — happened to be in that region and was hired by the engineers who were moving the Thunder Stone to St. Petersburg."

The Thunder Stone, Saul suddenly remembered, was the name of the pub.

Saul and Petro got up from the table and moved to the bar where Petro took a small framed picture off the wall.

"Yes, I name my place after the Thunder Stone. Here, you see it here, an extremely rare thing — a single stone, a monolith, weighing more than 1,500 tons. It was discovered embedded in the marshlands around Lakhta, and the Empress, Catherine the Great, decided it would make the perfect pedestal for a statue of Peter the Great. My ancestor was one of the 400 men hired to move the stone to the sea."

Petro held the picture up to the light. Saul saw a wintry scene, a clearing in a familiar-looking spruce forest — it might have been in the woods above Birthlayn — where a colourful array of spectators watched as stonecutters scrambled over a gigantic boulder, wielding their hammers and chisels on it even as it was being dragged along the frozen ground, teams of men straining at the enormous capstans as the giant stone inched its way along a track improvised from huge pieces of timber.

Petro pointed to a figure in the crowd.

"Here you see Catherine the Great. She has come to see this work of hers in progress. Also, you see there are no animals in the work. Only men. It was nine months to move the stone 6 kilometres. About 150 metres each day."

"That's ... amazing," said Saul.

"At the sea, the stone was put on a barge and shipped to the city. It was, as you say, an amazing accomplishment. My people decided to stay in the region afterwards because there was much acclaim for the men involved in this thing, even if they were gypsies and Jews."

Saul grew quiet, awed by the tale of the empress and her grand design, and by the notion of the unnamed and unremembered workers whose lives had been ennobled by the enterprise.

"I see you are a dreamer, Saul."

Petro had spoken the words kindly. "You are a large dreamer. I have a gift for seeing such things and I saw this in you right away."

Saul smiled wryly. "My father says I'm a dreamer," he said.

"Yes, but I do not think he means this as a compliment. I do."

They moved back to the table where the sleeping Ben now emitted small wheezing noises.

"Saul, listen to me. This place you come from, Birthlayn, I have seen it."

"You've been to Birthlayn?"

"No, but I have *seen* it. We gypsies have our ways. There is a stone there, a very large stone. No, it is not the Thunder Stone — that is rare beyond words — but it is one, it is whole, and for this reason it is important. I tell you, Saul Dade, in the place of this stone there is a treasure and it will help you obtain everything you seek."

...

The ride to the police station after the knife incident was shadowy and strange. After waiting all day for Chancey to come back, Jason finally sat alone and silent in the back of the police car watching the bits of yellow on the policeman's uniform float eerily in the gloom.

At first, Chancey had resisted the idea of Jason going to make a statement — the car would be ready in the morning and he was afraid of getting tangled up in something that might stop them from getting back on the road — but in the end he relented and even picked up the phone to make the call. He promised to wait up until Jason got back.

Once they got to the police station Jason and the officer went into a small room and Jason started to cry. The officer just sat and watched and didn't speak even though Jason cried for quite a long time. For Jason, this kind of crying had started at the university. It always took him by surprise when it happened but he'd learned not to mind it so much since he found he usually felt better afterwards.

"You okay?" the officer asked at last.

"I'm tired, that's all."

"You sure you want to keep travelling with this fellow?"

"Oh yes. I have to."

"Well, you don't have to. We could help you go home, you know."

"That would be the wrong thing to do. I've got to go to North City."

"Why is that now?"

"I'm supposed to meet a man there."

"Really. What man is that?"

Jason hesitated.

"He's not a man *exactly*. He's my brother. My brother George. He's waiting for me there."

The officer looked searchingly at Jason, then shook his head. "All right," he said, "I won't get in touch with your parents then, since there's no point in making them worry. And you're *sure* you're not hurt."

Jason wiped his cheeks decisively with the heels of his hands. The scratch on his back from the accident was stinging under his shirt but he resisted the urge to try and soothe it somehow.

"I'm okay," he said. "I really am."

"I want you to make a statement and we will have a word with Elvis Murphy. I don't know if we will charge him since you're not prepared to stick around. You should know that he's gotten on with this kind of nonsense before, but his bark is always worse than his bite."

"All I want is for you to know what happened," said Jason.

Jason gave and signed his statement and the officer brought him back to the bar.

The next day, at last, they made it to the ferry. The eighteen-hour crossing was long and uncomfortable. Chancey, without even a blanket, slept like a dog on the floor. Jason managed to doze in one of the recliners. The two of them squinted against the light when they came up on deck next morning to see the Nova Scotia shoreline appear in the bluish dawn. Jason was struck by the grassy meadows and banks of reddish-brown clay that sloped into the sea. It all seemed so tame and reasonable to him. The shores of Nova Scotia looked like a manicured lawn compared to the rough cliffs they'd left behind in Port aux Basques.

Chancey wanted to keep driving once they got on shore. "But no more sleeping at the wheel," he said with a sheepish grin. "Not good for the health." They went flat out all day and had crossed into New Brunswick by nightfall when they pulled up to a motel.

In the motel room, Chancey grabbed the remote and lay on the bed. Jason was extremely restless and knew that sleep would be impossible. He decided to go for a walk. Over his shoulder he heard Chancey call, "Be careful out there," then stepped into the night.

...

One August evening in Birthlayn, the air unusually warm and still, little Jasie decided to go for a walk up the meadow alongside the clean brook. He tried for trout in a couple of his favourite places, caught two with his bare hands and let them go. After imagining himself discovering a cure for cancer among the nameless flowers that grew along the bank, he wandered into a bed of purple thistles and lay down. He looked up at the blue sky and pondered the eternal cold of outer space and thought of God out there somewhere, watching, wondering what to do with His troubled world. Then he closed his eyes, went inward, and watched the colours rise and turn and drift and fade in the blackness behind his eyelids. In the distance a chainsaw whined, a dog barked, an axe split wood, a mother called her child to supper, a car made its careful way up the road; it all seemed so peaceful, so perfect, so right.

That evening Ana had her sewing machine set up at the kitchen table, and she watched her boy through the window as he drifted back down the meadow. She watched until he passed from view and then went back to her work. She did not see when he slipped on a rock crossing the brook and fell on his arse into the water. Oh, he could have cried, he was so disappointed in himself. His socks and sneakers and pants and underwear were all soaked. His mother never liked it when the boys came home in wet clothes. How unfair it was that a bawling out, and possibly even a trimming, should mark the close of such a beautiful day! It took a long time for him to walk the rest of the way, the daylight fading by the time he finally got back to the house.

He opened the kitchen door and saw his mother working her sewing machine in the dusky light. She turned a silver wheel with one hand, trod on a black pedal, then steered the fabric into the thrumming needles. Jasie was always nervous of those needles, afraid they would grab his mother's fingers and mash them into a bloody pulp.

Night had crept in so gradually that Ana hadn't yet thought to turn on a light. She looked up at the shadowy figure of her boy lingering in the doorway. Jasie was sure she knew his clothes were wet and dreaded what was to come. But, "Did you have a nice walk?" was all she said.

"Yes, Mom."

"Take off your boots now and come on in, like a good boy."

His mother always said take off your *boots* when he came indoors, no matter if it was sneakers, or rubbers, or pissquicks, or whatever it was he had on, so he took off his sneakers, crossed the kitchen and laid them behind the stove. His socks left a trail of wet footprints. There was no fire in the stove, though he could feel a residual heat in the hot water boiler. He peeled off the wet socks and hung them over the pipe connecting the boiler to the stove. His feet suddenly felt clean and refreshed.

"Go change your pants now, Jasie," she said, and that's when he knew there was no reason to be afraid.

A few minutes later he came out of the room and noticed the wet footprints had vanished. He stood at the side of the stove away from his mother and they talked, quietly, to each other for what seemed like hours. And for the very first time, Jasie thought he could hear the accents of her distant French ancestors fall from her lips in syllables so delicate it seemed they might crack and splinter on their way to him across the dusky light. And during the talk he somehow came to understand what he had in some sense always known but had never fully absorbed before; that his mother *loved* him, probably beyond anything he could imagine; an occasional swat on the behind or a harsh word or two as she went about her work could never change that.

From then on he was a little braver about venturing into the world.

...

Outside the motel, the night air was fresh and clean, heavy with expectation. There had been a light fall of rain and Jason could see the colours of the blinking neon sign reflected in the black shiny surface of the highway. Except for the odd passing car, there wasn't another light in sight, even the stars were strangely obscured. Still, Jason sensed he was close to some kind of town. He'd been amazed all day at the enormous distances between the neighbouring farms — the houses were miles apart! How could children play with their friends? How could you ever round up a softball team to go to the Groves on a summer afternoon? Or a posse to go swimming in the Cove?

New Brunswick, he decided, must be a lonely place to live.

After walking beside the highway for a half an hour or so, Jason noticed a silver shimmer above a copse of trees and saw a worn footpath trailing over a bank. He wandered through the copse and came upon a trailer park illuminated with street lights. There were no sidewalks, just gravel walkways following the bend of a single paved street. The trailers hunched on their small lots like perfectly respectable citizens, their neatly matched vinyl windows, like robotic eyes, emitting the soft yellow glow of domesticity. Each was fronted by a pathetic patch of lawn with an occasional small tree and, in one case, a white picket fence. Gleaming cars and trucks with their headlight eyes and grinning grillwork mouths seemed waiting and eager to be pressed into service.

The bend in the road deepened and he came upon a playground: a gravel lot with red and yellow monkey bars, a swing set, and a green plastic slide in the form of a huge frog that admitted youngsters via its rear and vented them on its large red tongue. Most blinds were drawn, some half-raised, others raised completely, yet Jason never spotted a human. He imagined the whole thing was an abandoned movie set.

Some of the owners had built wooden stoops, decorated them with flower pots and the odd gnome. Jason stopped in front of one with a small dome light on above the door. This gave it a slight welcoming edge so he walked onto the stoop and knocked. The woman who answered was about sixty, he figured, seeing her tightly drawn and dyed-black hair, her eyeglass frames encrusted with fake jewellery. She wore a pink sweater, modest round-toed shoes, and a pleated grey skirt. Jason was immediately drawn to her by a curious sense of recognition.

He hadn't planned anything specific to say but his words came easily, as if from a movie script.

"Listen, lady," he said, enjoying the casual gangsterism of the phrase, "I'm not an alcoholic or anything, but if I don't get a drink soon, I don't know what I'm gonna do."

The trailer park lady went inside and left the door open behind her. Jason hung back on the stoop until he heard her sing out, "I'm in here." He stepped inside to a tidy little kitchen with a shiny linoleum floor and pine cabinetry. A small florescent light was on over the stove. He found her in the living room sitting demurely in an oversized armchair. The living room set was flowery, mostly vivid orange, the carpet a solid green. A triangular bottle of scotch stood beside an expensive-looking glass on the coffee table.

"Single malt," she said. "Good for what ails ya." Then, she added rather loudly, as if the comment were meant to be heard by someone in a bedroom down the hall, "My son is gone to bed early. He might come out in a minute to say hello. Or he might not." Then she lowered her voice dramatically and said, "Maybe we shouldn't disturb him. Yes, I think that would be best."

Jason poured himself a reasonable drink and asked for water. She got up and went to the kitchen, he heard the hiss of the tap, and she came back holding a little ceramic jug. "There you go. You should have everything you need there now. Don't ask for food because I don't have any food. That one in there" — she pointed toward the bedroom as she resumed her seat— "ate every last morsel we had for supper."

Jason knew they were alone in the trailer, that the son in the back was a fiction, but he didn't let on. The woman was being kind to him and that was all that mattered.

The scotch was vitally reassuring on its way down.

"I've been in a car accident," he said, "and a fellow attacked me with a knife yesterday."

She grimaced and sipped from her glass.

"The guy who's driving me only has one lung."

"Sounds like he's not much of a driver."

"He's all I got."

"That's too bad. Where you headed?"

"Up north."

"What for?"

"There's this man I've got to see."

"What man is that now?"

He liked this woman, her gentle questions.

"I don't know, really. I only met him once before, for like a minute, last year in a bar in St. John's. All I know right now is that it's important to meet him again."

"Did he invite you to come for a visit?" The woman nursed her Scotch in a dry crepey hand. It looked like she was drinking it straight.

"No. But he knows I'm coming. I'm not sure if he's in the north, really. He could be in Montreal or Toronto, or some place like that."

"Then why go north?"

"I think it's where I'm supposed to go right now."

"And how do you know that?"

"I just do."

"I see. And what are you going to do when you find this man?"

"I'll know that when I find him. He wants us to meet."

The woman nodded her head thoughtfully, slipped a cigarette from a pack on the table, lit it and took a big draw. She tossed the lighter on the table with a clatter.

"So," she said, "what do you *think* is going to happen when you two meet?"

"I'm going to prove myself."

"Ah. I see. Prove what, exactly?"

"I'm going to prove I'm The One."

"The One?"

"The One who's a perfect match for him."

"I see."

"I almost pulled it off last year when I was at university, but something went wrong."

"What went wrong?"

"I'm not sure. But this time I know I'll get it right."

"I must say it all sounds terribly exciting."

"It is. It's a kind of game, you see. Last year I lost everything and now I'm going to win it all back."

"So, you're going to make a comeback."

Jason smiled. She understood perfectly.

"That's my speciality, you see."

"The comeback?"

"The long shot. I'm going to take the longest long shot in the history of the world. I don't know yet what it will be, except that it will be something amazing."

"Well, isn't that ... something."

"Yes, it is."

The woman stubbed out her half-smoked cigarette, an extravagance which Jason also found quite movie-like, then stood up.

"Where are you staying?"

"At a motel down the highway."

"Maybe you should be getting back. Maybe your friend, the lousy driver, will be worried about you?"

Jason laid his glass on the coffee table and stood up too.

"It was kind of you to let me in. You're a very generous person."

She laughed and called again to the back room in that false voice. "Isn't that what *you* always say?

Generous to a fault." She lowered her voice again. "He'll be getting up any second now. You better go. Have a last quick one for the road."

Jason threw back a straight Scotch and felt the beneficial fire spreading through his body. Scotch. The Man would know all about Scotch.

"I'll be able to sleep now," Jason said in the entranceway. "Thank you. The world won't forget what you've done here tonight."

"I know," the woman said, and quietly closed the door on him.

Back at the hotel, he found Chancey stretched out watching TV. Jason undressed and kicked his way under the sheets. Chancey flicked off the television and sat in his underwear on the edge of his own bed smoking the day's last cigarette.

And Jason smiled to see the boyhood myth disproved; smoke was spewing forth from Chancey's right *and* left nostrils.

...

When Jasie Dade was a boy his father could be away working in North City for weeks or even months at a time. So it was a pretty special night when Daddy got home and the family gathered in the kitchen to watch him empty one of his large suitcases on the floor. It always contained an impressive collection of minor industrial supplies: pocketknives, wrenches, an assortment of screwdrivers, rolls of electric and fibreglass tape, boxes of nails and screws, various kinds of sealants and putties, a hammer or two, various grades of sandpaper, a hack saw, insulation strips for doors and windows, trowels and putty knives, woollen socks and work gloves, toques and balaclavas for the freezing outdoors, dust masks, protective goggles, welding glasses and a welding torch, hefty flashlights, batteries, smaller flashlights, mysterious lubricants, pastes and oils, a level, a helmet, a square, and on and on and on. Saul would display and/or demonstrate each item in turn with evident enjoyment and pride. He wanted to give the youngsters some idea of the scope and magnitude of the hydroelectric project he was working on, a hint of the sumptuous and extravagant wealth that made it possible, and of his small role in it all, his tiny but significant role in the march of progress.

It was on such a night that Saul did what he'd never done before: he talked about the war. It was the first and only time Jasie ever heard his father speak in detail of how his ship had been torpedoed by the Germans one morning at sea and how he'd been forced to jump into the freezing waters of the Atlantic and swim for his life. That night Jasie caught yet another glimpse of the long strange life that sat in his father's back pocket.

The woodstove ticked its warmth and an amber glow filled the kitchen as the questions leapt from him and Georgie. Sarah, too young to be up, had fallen cosily asleep in her mother's arms.

"What was it like to be in the water, Father?"
"Were you alone?"
"Was it cold?"
"How far did you swim?"
"Were you scared?"

And they quieted instantly when Saul resumed his story.

"I was alone," he said, looking deeply into something that only he could see, "when I was in the water ... and all I did ... I looked around and I said to myself ... I'm here now ... I'm here and there's nothing I can do about it ... except wait. The only thing I *can* do is stay calm ... stay calm and wait ... and soon someone will find me. And, before long, someone did."

And Jasie knew in his heart that the amazing story his father told was true because his father had never, not even when he'd had a lot to drink, talked like that before. And Jasie also knew the story was true because Saul had never spoken of it again. In fact, after a few days, Jasie hardly thought of it either. It belonged to the distant unknowable past, and the present was pretty much all he had time for in his eager growing-up little boy's life.

...

Not long after he got back from his trip to Ballater, Saul Dade came down the gangway of the ship and saw a tight cluster of men on the harbour apron. Something feverish in their manner and their short excited cries told him they were watching a fight. Sure enough, when he got there he saw two of his shipmates sprawled and tussling on the grainy concrete. One, obviously the older of the two, held another much younger-looking fellow in a fierce headlock. The young fellow thrashed and writhed and kicked to throw off his tormentor, but the older man hung on with bulldog-like persistence. Finally, choked and exhausted, the young fellow cried uncle. His opponent jumped to his feet and promptly inspired cries of "Christ, b'y!" and "Holy fuck!" by giving the young fellow a parting boot in the face. Saul was vaguely sickened by the sound and by the way the beaten man covered his face with a muffled scream. The victor, grim but resolute, rolled his eyes at Saul as if to say, what a goings on! and went back on board ship. The others drifted away as their vanquished shipmate rose unsteadily from the pavement and wiped the blood from his face.

The victor's name was Mitchell Howell. In the first week of training Mitchell had hung his hammock from the ceiling pipes right beside Saul's. Perhaps because they were both past the average age of the seamen on board, they'd been favourably inclined toward one another. They made pleasant conversation and shared a taste for staying in their bunks to read for hours even when shore leave was available.

"Why'd you do that?" Saul asked later when they were once again perched in their hammocks.

"They were giving me a hard time, the young ones, calling me old timer and skipper and so on … I can't have that … It's going to be hard enough to get through this war in one piece. I thought it best to give one of them a good beating to shut the whole crowd of them up. Hopefully, it's done the trick."

"What about …?"

"He's young. He'll get over it."

"But in the face like that?"

"I used the side of my boot, not the toe. The sound is bad, but there's no real damage. The fellow still has all his teeth. Basically, I gave him a bloody nose. It could have been much worse."

Saul smiled, quietly exhilarated. So this is how a man deals decisively with a problem.

"Why him, though?" Saul asked.

Mitchell chuckled. "He just happened to be the one to open his mouth at the wrong time, though it doesn't hurt that his name is Squires."

"Squires?"

"Maybe he's related to that arsehole Prime Minister who left Newfoundland in such bad shape that we had to give up the government. If so, serves him doubly right." Saul had never heard anyone speak about Newfoundland politics quite as personally as Mitchell Howell tended to do. To Saul, politics had always been a thing that just happened, as inevitable, and indifferent to him, as falling rain.

The two became friends after that. Mitchell told him that he'd recently become engaged to a British woman named Dorothy Thompson. It was his plan — one she'd already agreed to — to bring her home to Newfoundland after the war. His parents ran a successful farm just outside St. John's where there'd always be a job for Mitchell until his larger ambitions in law and politics came to fruition. And Mitchell Howell, Saul quickly discovered, had no shortage of plans and ambition.

With Mitchell, Saul found himself for the first time drawn into conversation about his little country's place in the greater world. He'd always thought of Newfoundland in the same static unchanging way he thought of Birthlayn. But Mitchell had other, much more interesting ideas: "You take it from me, Saul, Newfoundlanders have had enough of this Government by Commission we're living under now. I mean, okay, it may have had its purpose but it's basically a dictatorship and once this war is over there's going to be no taste for that sort of thing anymore. Meanwhile, there's been a friendly invasion by the Americans so there's plenty of cash around. People are going to want an elected government. That means we're going to have to create a whole new civil service and *that's* going to create lots of opportunities for smart fellows like you and me." Saul was immensely flattered by the suggestion that he could be part of these great and future plans and would smile to imagine himself going to work one day in a government office carrying an attaché case and wearing a suit and tie. Nagged by feelings of inadequacy, he protested his lack of formal education. "Night courses," Mitchell said, as if the solution to every problem was as straightforward as giving a young sailor a much-needed kick in the head. "Start taking them as soon was the war's over. You'll have your high school before you know it. By then I'll be elected to the House of Assembly and I'll see to the rest." And Saul would grin in spite of himself at this display of easy confidence. He loved Mitchell and everything about him and found it hard to fathom why such a man would choose to be serious friends with someone as unconnected and underprivileged as himself.

Saul was mightily impressed by Dorothy, as well. She wore red lipstick, smoked cigarettes, wore pleated skirts and, all in all, struck him as an English version of the American actress Jane Russell. On top of that she was a journalist who wrote for a small-town British newspaper. Mitchell himself had been writing a column about his war experiences for a newspaper back home until his superiors insisted he stop for fear of a security breach. Mitchell was miffed because the column was laying down track for his political career after the war. Still, all things considered, it was clear that Mitchell and Dorothy would have a tremendous future together. And why, thought Saul, shouldn't he hitch his wagon to their bright particular star?

...

In bed at last, Jason closed his eyes and watched a small distant ember emerge from the blackness and begin to move, slowly at first and then more playfully, back and forth across the field of his inner vision. Back and forth it bounced, left right up down, as if penned in by an invisible border. Soon his eyes came completely to rest, though he followed the ember still, but with an awareness that lay somewhere behind his eyes.

Then the spark exploded, silently, in a bright orange blaze which eventually faded into a field of flickering white static — snow, his father used to call it when the television screen broke, slamming his hand repeatedly on the console in an effort to bring back whatever program had dissolved beneath it — and Jason watched the flickering bits come together slowly to form a single silver glow and it was *as* this silver glow that he felt himself rise from the bed and travel along what seemed an undulating highway of light. He accelerated to a breathless speed, then slowed, and slowed, and eventually came to rest over a large, well-lit, beautifully appointed room. He saw a large unmade bed with rumpled linens and a pair of French doors that opened onto a small wrought iron balcony.

An elegant beach house? A mountain chalet? It was difficult to tell since the place existed in perfect silence, surrounded by its own cloud-like aura. An Amsterdam apartment? A Montreal hotel suite? It didn't matter, really. The main thing was that the place held within it the definite presence of The Man.

Jason opened his eyes to moonlight filtering in narrow beams through the blinds.

He was on the right track.
At last.

...

Little Jasie Dade once saw a heifer get loose in a slaughterhouse. A most amazing thing. The slaughterhouse looked like a pretty little roadside cabin — bright red felt on a peaked roof, white clapboard with red trim — standing all alone in a meadow. It belonged to George Breen, who owned the local store. Mr. George kept a few cattle himself and slaughtered anyone else's for hire. A small fenced enclosure stood beside the gravel path which led to the slaughterhouse from the road. It was there they dumped the remains of the slaughtered beasts. Jasie always stopped to take a look when it was full of maggots. If he listened carefully enough, he could hear them, seething.

Inside the slaughterhouse there was nothing but a grey concrete floor and a heavy brass ring beside the drainage hole. Little Jasie often stood around in his overalls, peeking through the legs of the small crowd that gathered to watch as the beasts, usually cattle, were readied for slaughter. The men would tie a rope, usually around the horns, slip the rope through the brass ring and pull the animal's head down next to the drainage hole. Then came the hammer blow, which buckled its knees; they slit its throat and shed its lifeblood into the hole. Sometimes, they rooted around in the throat wound with a knife hoping to puncture the heart. Once, George Breen, having removed the heart, showed everyone the slit his knife had made.

Jasie was always struck by the prismatic dazzle in the dead animal's eyes.

The fact the white heifer had no horns must have allowed it to get loose. The rope slipped. The next thing anyone knew the heifer was running wild inside the slaughterhouse, trying to burst out of that small cold room. And here's the amazing thing. It bolted toward the open door and Jasie thought for a heartbeat that it was going to get free until George Breen jumped in the doorway with his arms spread wide, threw himself right in front of that fear-crazed heifer, and Jasie thought that the heifer would just knock George Breen down and barrel through the small crowd of onlookers into the meadow and escape. He also thought it very brave, even foolish, of George Breen to stand in the way like that. But, as it turned out, George Breen won. In the next heartbeat, the heifer balked, turned from the door and ranged, defeated, inside the slaughterhouse until someone got the rope on it again, the men got re-organised, and they finished the job.

Little Jasie couldn't bear to watch the killing that day. He felt too sorry for the heifer. It got loose, but it didn't get away. All the way home he kept thinking that if *he* ever had a chance like that, a slim doorway to freedom staring him in the face and nowhere else to turn, he'd go through, and he swore, too, that he wouldn't let anyone, no matter who they were, stand in his way.

September

The youngsters of Birthlayn had covered a lot of territory that summer: from the cliffs to the marshes; from the High Mountains to the Downs; from the gulls' nests on Kitty's Pinch to the rookery on Black Head (where Georgie climbed all the way up and stole his pet crow from the nest); miles and miles of terrain covered, always on foot, or on imaginary horses with names like Trigger and Bullet and Lightning, riders' tongues clacking quietly in their cheeks as their steeds leapt across brooks and over fences, cantered along gravel roads and open meadows.

And Georgie's dog, Susie, was with them every step of the way.

Saul Dade was generally against household pets, but when Georgie brought Susie home as a pup the dog quickly figured out that Saul, not Georgie, was really the one in charge and would literally dance for joy every time Saul walked into the house. Saul's heart was soon won over and he came to love Susie as much or more than the youngsters did. But out gallivanting, Susie was still Georgie's dog and she was with them that Labour Day weekend in September, their last real day of summer before returning to school, when they were trooping across the shorn meadows of the Downs to see if the American pillboxes had once again filled with rain from the night before.

The Americans had built the concrete bunkers called pillboxes on the Downs to serve as lookouts for their naval base. Only the concrete walls of the hollowed-out structures remained, remnants of an unknown war and an endless curiosity to the roaming youngsters. After a heavy rain the pillboxes would fill with water the colour of milky tea and, occasionally, small treasures floated to the surface.

It struck little Jasie as comical at first when Susie ran ahead of the pack and sprang off the parapet into the pillbox, belly-flopping into the water. The others thought it funny too as she swam around and around, but it wasn't long before the laughter stilled and the horrible truth set in. Susie was going to drown before their eyes. She was too far down in the bunker to be able to climb out by herself and there was no one among them big and strong enough to reach in and pull her out. Panic set in as they watched Susie swim from one end of the bunker to the other, tiring, scratching at the concrete, trying in vain to climb out. She even tried to climb onto a cluster of floating driftwood which, time after time, sank beneath her weight.

Then Georgie started taking off his boots, determined to get into the bunker and keep his dog afloat. Jasie knew this was a very bad idea because his brother would quickly be in the same predicament as the dog. He pictured Susie climbing onto Georgie's back the way she was trying to climb onto those floating bits of wood. He imagined claw marks on Georgie's back and desperation on his freckled face as, perhaps even before Susie, he was swallowed by the muddy water.

Georgie's shirt was off now and he was sitting on the edge of the bunker ready to leap when Jasie heard a voice and suddenly he was running. It was his own voice he heard above the pounding of his heart, calling to some bigger boys he'd spotted in the distance.

"Help! Susie's drowning, Susie's drowning ... come and help ... ." He ran as fast and roared as loud as ever he could. And they came. And the dog's salvation was ridiculously, miraculously, simple. Billy Breen, a boy of sixteen with golden curls and a strong right arm, leaned over the parapet, grabbed Susie by the scruff of the neck and, as easy as pie, lifted her right out of the water. Droplets slid from her tawny coat as she sailed through the air, then landed with a thump on the ground. She shook herself from head to tail, then trotted off as if the whole thing had never happened. So much disaster averted by the grace of one boy's arm. A cheer went up for Billy Breen.

Jasie cheered aloud for Billy Breen that day, but he was cheering in his heart for Georgie. Of course, he would've been mad as hell if Georgie had died trying save the stupid dog, yet he couldn't help but love his brother for being the only one to act in a moment when everyone, himself included, had been paralysed with fear.

...

George Dade had last seen his brother on a visit home from North City at Easter. He'd heard from his parents about the disastrous and abandoned first year at university, and had gathered by the gossip trickling up from Birthlayn that Jason wasn't exactly himself.

Though none of it prepared him for what he saw once he did get home.

George had always been the stocky one, so it was disturbing to see the younger brother, who'd always been so clean-faced and thin, shuffling around the house with a paunch and a beard. Added to that, Jason had barely acknowledged George's presence and refused all invitations to go out, preferring instead to spend the Easter holiday pretty much as he'd spent the winter months, as George understood it, sitting on his bed smoking cigarettes, or watching TV in the living room with a faraway look in his eyes.

So it came as a bit of a shock when George opened his bunkhouse room door in early September and found Jason standing there with his eyes on fire, pale, clean-shaven and thinner than he'd been in years. It was impossible to tell if things had gotten better or worse.

"So. Ya made it," George said. "C'mon in."

Jason walked in and dropped his duffle on the floor.

"I ran into Chancey earlier. He said you were in a car accident?"

"Chancey flipped the car. Nobody got hurt."

"Chancey. That fucking idiot. Why'd the old man make you go with him anyway?"

"The old man didn't *make* me do anything."

Jason shrugged out of his coat. "I need to get some sleep," he said.

"Sure. You can use my bed once I start nights, but for now …"

"The floor's fine."

"Well, take a blanket, at least …"

"The floor's fine."

Jason lay on the bare floor facing a baseboard heater and settled his coat over himself.

"Take a fucking pillow, at least," George said, throwing one at him.

"Thanks." Jason put the pillow under his head and George heard him say, "Can you loan me two hundred dollars?"

"Sure," said George.

"Good."

George got up early the next morning and took the bus to the mine. When he got back at six-thirty North City was already getting dark and it didn't seem strange to find Jason still sound asleep on the floor. But when he climbed into bed that night, slept, woke up the next morning, went to work and came home again to find Jason still sleeping with his face to the wall, he found it perplexing.

...

Saul Dade was asleep in his hammock when the first torpedo hit. On impact, he sat bolt upright and slammed his head into the cast iron ceiling. Dazed and hurt, he rolled out to the floor where he struggled to keep his feet and get his bearings. He saw Mitchell's empty hammock and remembered that his friend was on watch. He heard the call to abandon ship, felt the severe list, and knew that they were sinking.

He ran to find his muster station with just enough presence of mind to register the rapid, ordered responses of his shipmates, feeling strangely elated to be one of them, doing his part in holding, even under fire, to the rigorous discipline of the ship. On deck, he discovered a bright sunny day, drastically unsuited to the events unfolding around him. The ship listed sharply astern, the thick sweet stench of burning oil singed his nostrils, his shipmates swarmed the deck as if suddenly thrown into a frenzied game of schoolyard tag, in the distance he glimpsed the dark outline of a U-boat conning tower; it would be his one and only enemy sighting during the war.

At the crowded muster station he found that his lifeboat had been blown to bits. He saw other lifeboats being lowered, most of them full, still others aloft with crowds of men waiting to board. He sensed a decision looming: jump overboard and swim as far as possible from the ship to avoid being pulled down in the undertow or join in the frantic search for a seat on another lifeboat. The second torpedo made up his mind. He made for the railing. One of his mates fell to the deck in front of him. Saul had never seen anyone fall like that, so utterly without resistance, the intricate framing of the body instantly abandoned to gravity. He stopped and turned the body over, surprised by its dead weightiness. It was Squires. The small cut on his nose left by Mitchell's boot was slightly scabbed over. It had almost healed. On the right temple, a small red slit where the shrapnel had made its entry. Other than that the poor young fellow just looked surprised. Then a dark pool started to form on the deck below his head.

With the whiff of blood in his nostrils, Saul leapt to the ship's rail, climbed outside it and, with his arms outstretched like benign useless wings, jumped. He felt the wind rip the round cap from his head as if in some wild joyous celebration. He sucked in and released as much air as he could several times, trying to time it so that his lungs would be completely full at the instant his body knifed feet-first into the freezing cold water. He sank down, down, down, a fierce band around his chest tightening more and more until he finally stopped and hung suspended in the cold dark. The desire for air was maddening. He struck out for the surface and when he broke through he sucked the first blast of it so hungrily it seemed the bright blue sky, clouds and all, would be drawn down inside him as well.

He swam as fast as he could to escape the shadow of the ship and the black oil dispensing from her wounds. He came to clear water and stopped long enough to remove his boots and shake off his heavy pants. He didn't look back after that, just kept swimming, his arms and breath labouring and his heartbeat thundering in his ears. *Keep going*, he repeated and repeated, *not far enough yet, not far enough yet to be safe. I will not die. I will not die. I will not die.*

At last, exhausted by his efforts and the burden of his terror, he stopped swimming and looked around. The ship, he knew, was doomed. A last few souls were leaping from her guardrails, lifeboats bobbed in the distance, making their way to small dark figures waving their arms in the water. He was startled to find himself alone.

His breath slowed and a mysterious calm settled on him. He was cold and shivering, but no colder than he'd sometimes been on his long swims out of Princeton or Paddy's Cove. He realised he hadn't taken a lifejacket.

He could tell even at a distance that most of the men in the water and those being pulled to the relative safety of the lifeboats were wearing them, but he felt secure all the same, confident in his own ability to stay afloat. He remembered how, as a boy, swimming, especially in the sea, had meant freedom to him, an escape, a liquid version of flight.

He saw that his boyhood had prepared him for this moment of trial. He would bide his time, and they would come for him. He would board a lifeboat and, soon after, an escort ship, and from there he would find a way back into his life.

All he had to do, all he *could* do for now, was stay calm and wait.

...

Miss Martina Crockwell, wiry and efficient, taught Grades One to Three at the Birthlayn two-room school where she ruled with an iron hand. Since the day she'd arrived everyone from the parents to the school superintendent had ordered her to be strict. And so she was, though her austerity was largely a pose since the students were, by and large, well-behaved. They were smart and studious as well, mostly the girls, as a rule. And then there was the exception that made the rule, a little boy named Jasie Dade.

What could she say about little Jasie Dade? In Grade Three he wrote cursive with a fine steady hand; his scribblers were regularly stamped with red and blue stars that denoted excellence on every page; his homework was always done, tidily and correctly; he went home every day with a library book in his schoolbag —

mostly detective stories like *The Hardy Boys* and *The Bobbsey Twins,* even the female detective *Nancy Drew* when there was nothing else available — and he often brought them back read by the next morning.

Even when he was getting the strap, which all the children, including the girls, occasionally did, little Jasie Dade lent some dignity to the proceedings. He offered his palms willingly and with great composure. Some of the children were given to crying and even pulling their hands away at the last second, which occasionally caused Miss Crockwell to strike herself on the leg, leaving her obliged to double the number of straps for the offending child. But that never happened with Jasie. He always took his medicine like a little man.

Even Jasie's bad behaviours were good in a way. For example, turning around in his desk and talking out of turn usually stemmed from his enthusiasm for some story that he was dying to tell or that she'd accidently set off in him by the current lesson. Like the other day when she'd used measures of weight to illustrate addition and she looked up from her desk to see that three or four of the children had stopped doing their assigned sums to hear what Jasie was saying. Miss Crockwell simply couldn't let that go.

"Jasie Dade."

"Yes, Miss."

"Are you talking?"

"Yes, Miss."

That was another thing; the young fellow never told a lie, not even to get out of a strapping.

"Well, perhaps you could share what you're saying with the whole class."

Innocent of her sarcasm, he carried on eagerly.

"I was talking about what I read last night in my encyclopedia, Miss, the one my Aunt Agnes sent us from the United States, about this man, his name was Damocles, I think is how you say it, Miss, and he was Greek, and he was best buddies with the king, you know, and he was always saying to the king that it must be great to be the king, you know, because the king has such a great life an' all, and so one day the king says, 'Look, I'll switch places with you, Damocles, and at the feast tomorrow you can sit on my throne and I'll sit in your place and you'll be treated just like me and we'll see how you like it.' The man said that would be great and the next day the king had everything set up so that this fellow, Damocles, could sit on the throne and have the best of food and drink and servants waiting on him hand and foot and he was having a great time until he looked up over his head and saw this big heavy sword hanging by a hair, *one hair from a horse's tail*, Miss, and it looked like it would snap off any second and come down and kill him and that's when he understood that it isn't easy or even nice to be king after all because if you're king there's always going to be someone wantin' to kill you and take your place."

"I see. Well, that's very interesting, Jasie." Miss Crockwell reached inside her desk drawer for the strap. "I'm sure we're all delighted to know that. Now, come up here and hold out both your hands."

...

Between dreams and brief awakenings, Jason slowly recharged his batteries. He'd awakened several times to stare at the dusty baseboard heater radiating into his face but each time shut his eyes again and slept and slept until he had no idea what time of day or even what day it was anymore. When he woke up hungry, he knew it was time to get up. He rolled over to see George lying on the bunk reading a paperback novel. On the cover a half dozen wary cowboys were lassoing a wild stallion.

"Hey. Where do we eat?" Jason said, managing a soft smile.

"The dining hall." George held up a white card. "Meal ticket. For you."

"Thanks."

"Thought you were down for the count there, brother."

"Never fear." Jason stood up and crawled into his coat. "Where do people hang out around here?"

"The Pit, mostly."

"The Pit."

"The Snake Pit. Just around the corner from here."

"Hmm."

George laid his paperback aside, stood up, and counted ten twenty dollar bills into Jason's hand. He placed the meal ticket on top.

"That should do ya."

"I'll pay you back."

"Sure. When you can. It's all right."

"Where's the dining hall? I'm starving."

"C'mon."

The sunlight outside stabbed at Jason's eyes and it was five minutes before he could look up and take in his surroundings: first, the bunkhouses, long and low and grey, like henneries, then some tidy duplexes further along the street, a little strip mall above a slope, and, at the corner, a sullen brown building with irregular roof planes.

"That's The Gloo," said George, "as in Igloo. The Pit's in the basement."

"I'll check it out later," Jason said. "Let's go eat."

The dining hall, right across from the Igloo, was pretty much what you'd expect and reminded Jason of the dining halls at the university: cooks with bored faces turning greasy eggs; steel bins piled with bacon and sausage; a couple of giant toasters with rotating grills doing ten or a dozen slices at a time; silver tanks gushing chocolate and white milk so furiously the glass in your hand filled in two seconds flat.

Jason piled his plate with bacon, four eggs, and two slices of toast. As he ate, George sat across from him drinking coffee and smoking cigarettes. He watched his brother mop up the last bit of egg with a piece of toast and decided to broach what he judged to be a delicate matter.

"I can take you down to personnel tomorrow if you like," George said. "See what we can do about finding you a job."

"I've got a couple of things I have to do first," Jason replied, and went off looking for tea with a white mug dangling from his forefinger.

George was relieved. Jason would be a menace on a worksite. He likely never would, never *should*, get hired in this town. What was the old man thinking sending him up here, anyway?

Jason returned with his mug full of steaming tea and blew on it numerous times before taking a sip.

"No worries about the work situation," George said. "Whenever you feel you're ready, just let me know."

"I will." Jason rocked back on the hind legs of his chair and took a large look around. "I know you understand, George. It's going to take me a little while to figure out my next move."

...

Throughout September of his first year of junior high, Jasie Dade enjoyed the novelty of taking the bus to Princeton, that is, instead of simply walking down the road to the Birthlayn schoolhouse. Princeton, in general, had made his life a good deal more complicated. There were over thirty students in his Grade Seven class, instead of the usual ten or so in the classes at home. There was a uniform too, including a red jacket and necktie which, for the first time ever, made him feel quite manly. He was also constantly getting into fights. Oh, he'd always been a dab hand at fighting with his buddies in Birthlayn, but that was different. In Birthlayn, a fight meant you got a fellow into a headlock and held on or you wrestled him to the ground and sat on his chest until he cried uncle, but Princeton boys closed their fists and aimed for the face, and little Jasie was getting his share of bloody noses. Georgie was too busy fighting his own battles to take care of him. The one good thing about Princeton, apart from the bus rides, was that he didn't have to worry anymore about coming first in his class, since he assumed, with so many students, that it was simply beyond his reach.

For all these reasons Princeton, even three weeks into September, seemed a precarious place to venture into alone. But Jasie had just spent another long morning in the classroom aching to go to the bathroom. In Birthlayn he could take a dodge out behind the school at recess and relieve himself if he wanted to, or at home when he went there for lunch. But in Princeton these opportunities weren't available and there was a school rule besides that said you could only go to the bathroom once a day. Jasie often had his one turn used up by early morning. By lunchtime, it felt like there were razor blades in his kidneys. So on this particular day, to spare himself another agonizing afternoon squirming in his seat, he left the school grounds at lunchtime, ducked behind the Star Hall, and gratefully relieved himself on the beach rocks. Then he glanced up and saw the Esso gas station sign. He'd heard they were giving out the glossy new NHL schedules there, so he decided to scoot over and get one.

He pushed open the heavy glass door with both hands and sniffed a heady though not unpleasant mix of motor oil and gasoline. Two men in blue coveralls looked up from their conversation when the door banged shut. Through a glass partition he saw a car hoisted on a hydraulic jack being worked on by a mechanic with grease-blackened hands. One of the men, in clean blue coveralls with an Esso decal right above his heart, stepped to the counter.

"And what can I do for you today?" he said.

"..."

Jasie found there was something about the strangeness of the place and of the two men staring blankly at him as he struggled for his answer, that robbed him of his powers of speech. *Surely they knew why he was there.*

They had no chips or bars or gum or anything like that for sale; he certainly wasn't there to buy gas or have his car repaired, and besides, everyone and his dog had no doubt already been in looking for a hockey schedule. The man stared and stared and waited and the longer Jasie hesitated the more he felt his powers of speech slip away. He simply couldn't bring himself to put into words exactly what it was he'd come for. *A hockey schedule, a hockey schedule,* he said to himself. He realised how easy it would be to say aloud, yet remained incapable of doing so.

The second man was about to intervene when Mr. Esso put up his hand.

"No!" he insisted. "Let the boy *say* what it is he wants." Burning with humiliation, Jasie pulled open the door and left.

...

In North City, Jason took to hanging out a lot at the Snake Pit. He knew it was unlikely The Man would ever turn up in a place like that; in fact, he couldn't imagine the meeting ever taking place in North City at all, but something told him this was where he needed to be in order to find a way forward.

He was standing at the bar one night when a man strolled in, his small frame covered in thick snow pants and a down-filled parka, wearing a pair of clunking Kodiak boots with the laces undone. The fellow tossed his worn stocking cap on the bar and jabbed ineffectually at his wispy dry hair as if to restore some sense of order. Glancing into the barroom mirror, apparently satisfied, he ordered a rum and Coke.

He had a thin crusty look about him, reminding Jason of the actor, whose name he couldn't remember, who'd played the Martian in *My Favourite Martian*.

"How ya doin' young fella?" the man said, raising his glass.

"Best kind," said Jason.

They were the only two standing at the bar.

"Where you from?"

"Birthlayn," said Jason.

"I've heard of it," the fellow said, "though I've never been." He took a sip of his rum and Coke and, pinkie extended, laid it carefully on the bar. He put out his hand. "Name's Virgil. What's yours?"

"Jason."

"Jason! Good one. I've always liked that name."

"Why's that?"

"Jason and the Argonauts, you know, the quest for the Golden Fleece."

"Right. Of course."

Jason recalled the illustration of the golden fleece in his Aunt Agnes's encyclopedia.

"What's your last name, Jason?"

"Dade."

"Jason Dade. A jaded son!"

"What?"

"A jaded son. It's an anagram of your name."

"Anagram. Isn't that where you make a word out of the first letters of other words?"

"No, no, no. That's an acronym. They can be interesting too. An anagram makes a new word out of the existing letters of a word. Elvis lives, army of Mary ... am I getting through here?"

Jason's mind flew back to an article he'd read at university in *Rolling Stone* magazine.

"Mr. Mojo Risin'?"

"Jim Morrison! Exactly. That's very good. I'm impressed. So, *are* you a jaded son?"

"I don't think so," Jason replied.

"So, Mr. Jaded Son, what's your father's name?"

"Saul."

"Saul Dade. Hmm ... Daedalus! Now, isn't that interesting?"

Jason couldn't believe he'd never noticed that before. His mind returned to the encyclopedia, this time to the picture of a winged boy falling into the sea while the boy's father, also winged, hovered in the sky above and looked helplessly on.

"Daedalus was a master craftsman who built a pair of wings for himself and his son so they could escape the tyrannical King Minos who was holding them captive on the island of Crete," Virgil said.

"The boy flew too close to the sun," said Jason. "It melted the wax in his wings and he fell into the sea and drowned."

"That's right," said Virgil. "And the boy's name was ...?"

Jason reached deep into his recollection until it came.

"Icarus," he said.

Virgil slammed his hand down on the bar.

"Well, I'll be goddamned if someone with a proper education hasn't finally turned up in this place."

"Go fuck yourself, Verge," somebody called out to a chorus of laughs. Virgil toasted them grandly with a small bow and then turned back to Jason.

"Let's get the hell out of here," he said, with a sly wink. "I've got better stuff than this back in my room."

"Sure."

...

Saul Dade allowed himself to sink down, down, down, into a sun-shafted green world. He still had plenty of air in his lungs when he finally slowed and reversed his direction, swimming away from the darkness under his feet toward the sunlight shimmering on the surface. He broke the surface and took in the tidy stand of spruce and fir trees surrounding an almost perfectly circular pond. In the distance, Mitchell and Dorothy Howell stood on the veranda of their small country house waving him back to shore.

It was time for a bit of lunch.

When he emerged from the water moments later Dorothy handed him a big white towel. Saul dried himself in the sun as Mitchell, standing with a grin on his face in the shade of the veranda, held up a newspaper.

"I told you it was only a matter of time," he said. This had become something of a favourite phrase with Mitchell.

"What?"

Mitchell snapped the newspaper open and held it so Saul could read the headline.

"*Newfoundlanders To Hold National Convention.* So what?"

Despite Mitchell's encouragement, Saul had yet to acquire only a passing interest in politics.

"It's a gathering of representatives from every district in Newfoundland," Mitchell explained. "It will meet in St. John's next year to decide the political future of the country. Don't you see, Saul? It's only a matter of time now before we get our government back."

"How much time?" Saul asked, thinking on his dwindling savings.

"Now, Saul," said Dorothy, laying out sandwiches and tea on the veranda — she insisted on eating in the shade — "you worry too much about such things."

Saul climbed the steps and sat with his friends looking out at the pond and the trees and the harrowed fields that circled round behind them to the broader expanses of the farm. There was a wharf by the pond with a small rowboat tied up, and a wooden diving board anchored in a cradle of rocks. That morning Saul had executed an assortment of dives for Dot and Mitch, leaving them amazed that it was possible to do such things without the benefit of formal training.

"I'm not worried, Dot. I'm just being realistic," Saul said. "I don't know that I can hang on in town much longer. I was thinking Canada might be next for me."

"It might be next for all of us," Mitchell replied. "There's a small faction interested in having us join up, and I'm not so sure it's a bad idea."

"So the mountain may actually come to Mohammed, Saul," Dorothy said, "if you care to wait long enough."

Saul was getting tired of waiting. His dreams of marvellous post-war opportunities for veterans had been overly optimistic. Once he'd gotten back from overseas his only immediate reward, besides his service medals and some accumulated pay, was to be eligible for a settlement program in Exploits, in central Newfoundland, where ex-servicemen were offered plots of land and being trained as farmers. He'd started out with high hopes, but a hard first winter in a government-provided house without even basic amenities had convinced him that the initiative was headed for failure. He'd stuck it out for another growing season and moved back to St. John's in the fall. It wasn't long before Mitchell had come round with an invitation to visit the farm.

"Well, I've got to get a job," Saul said, sipping his tea. "I can't count on Mohammed *or* the mountain."

"Oh, ye of little faith," said Mitchell. His short laugh transformed into a sudden coughing fit, a thing Saul had noticed happening more and more as the war progressed, especially after their ship had gone down. Even though Mitchell had found his way into a lifeboat and avoided going into the water, it seemed the whole harrowing episode had nevertheless taken its toll. Mitchell's lifeboat was the one that had eventually rescued Saul. "Better you than me," Mitchell had said when Saul tumbled wet and freezing into the boat. And Saul knew that to be true. He and Dorothy exchanged worried looks as they waited for the coughing to subside.

"What he's trying to say," Dorothy said, "is that we have a plan for the future and we would like it to include you."

"Damn right," Mitchell croaked, still struggling to get his breathing under control. "Your recent adventures on the west coast have convinced my father that you might be enough of a farmer now to come and work for us. You can rent this place cheap from us and start night school right away. That'll see you through until something better comes along. It's only a matter of a year or two, Saul, and we're going to see some big changes. Wouldn't you like to be a part of it all? What do you say?"

Saul paused, then raised his teacup, pinkie in the air, and said, "I say," in a delightful imitation of Dorothy's accent, "that's a jolly good idea." And they all laughed cautiously, for Mitchell's sake, but happily, at the little joke.

...

It was the perfect time of day for a crucifixion. In another few minutes, if everything went as planned, the sun would be shining directly into the little saviour's face as he uttered his final words. The re-enactment was Georgie's idea and little Jasie had been flattered, at first, to be offered the leading role. But when he went around to the back of the house where his father kept the firewood and saw the heavy cross lying on the ground, he hesitated.

"Don't worry, Jasie," Georgie said, smiling. "We're not going to use nails."

His brother held up a ball of butcher's twine, knotted together bits he'd saved from the wrapped baloney slices his mother bought regularly at the store. So Jasie lay down and allowed himself to be tied by the wrists to the crossbeam. Multiple depictions of the crucifixion were going around and around in his head as he tried to figure out exactly what was missing from the cross, but when the boys raised it up and leaned him against the house, he knew. There was no footrest. The real saviour, for all his terrible suffering, always had support for his feet.

Jasie let out a cry of pain and Georgie nodded his approval. Then Georgie ordered one of the smaller boys to stand sombrely at the foot of the cross and look sad.

"You're the apostle John," he said to the boy. He pointed to another and handed him a wooden pole, "You're a Roman centurion."

"Ask for water," he ordered Jasie.

"I thirst," Jasie whimpered, just as they'd rehearsed it.

Georgie nodded at the centurion who stepped forward with the makeshift lance and a make-believe sponge. Jasie spat at the make-believe taste of vinegar.

"Now!" Georgie called, and the centurion thrust the lance at Jasie's side.

"Good," said Georgie, "now let your head fall to one side and say 'It is finished.'"

Jasie did this perfectly and to everyone's satisfaction, though by then it was all getting to be too much — his hands were swollen and purple and he was finding it more and more difficult to breathe. Georgie could see that Jasie had had enough but when he ordered the boys to lower the cross they found the upright had lodged itself firmly under a strip of clapboard and was stuck. The invisible weight on Jasie's chest was quickly becoming unbearable and he started to cry out in desperation.

Georgie grabbed their father's axe and chopped furiously away at the foot of the cross until it collapsed and their little saviour was lying safe on the ground breathing normally again.

It was a chilly walk back to the bunkhouses. Virgil's room was typical of what Jason had come to expect in North City: a shelf with a few spine-worn paperbacks, a curded soap dish, a frayed toothbrush in a dirty glass, a twisted toothpaste tube, two combs and a disposable razor in another glass, and two bottles of cheap aftershave, one blue, one green.

Virgil sat in a weathered captain's chair while Jason used the shaky folding chair opposite. A flea market-quality coffee table stood between them. The floor felt gritty underfoot as if ore dust from the mine had slowly been ground into the tiles. A filthy string mop leaned against a closet door. Four neatly stacked cardboard boxes had pride of place under the window. Virgil slipped his arms out of his parka, leaving it in place to cushion his chair, then leaned back and pulled a green triangular bottle out of one of the boxes.

"Scotch," he said, holding it toward Jason the way a waiter might display a bottle of wine. "The finest single malt there is. I keep my own supply. I'm forced to drink rum in that philistine bar." He jabbed a finger contemptuously in the direction of the Gloo and spun the metal cap off the bottle. He took a pair of plain drinking glasses from the windowsill and poured. "I've been watching you," he said, "watching you come and go at The Pit this last while and I think I see what you're about."

Jason grew very still.

"I know you can't talk about it, so I'm just going to say this, okay?" He leaned forward. "Just keep doing what you're doing and sooner or later you'll wind up exactly where you need to be."

"How do you know that?"

"From experience. I've been where you are and I think I know where you're headed."

"Okay."

They lifted their glasses and drank to their new understanding.

Virgil poured another. "You've got to learn to look at it like Ariadne's thread, if you know what I mean?"

"I don't know what you mean."

Virgil chuckled, took another sip. "So there *are* some gaps in your learning. Well, it was Ariadne's thread that got Theseus out of the labyrinth."

"Theseus? Like in *A Midsummer Night's Dream*? That Theseus?"

"Same guy, different story."

Jason listened then as Virgil poured the Scotch and told the story of Ariadne's thread, how Ariadne, the daughter of Minos, King of Crete, had fallen in love with Theseus, son of Aegeus, who was King of Athens when Theseus left for Crete to slay the Minotaur, a beast which every seven years killed seven of Athens' bravest sons and seven of her most beautiful maidens in a ritual sacrifice that had been arranged as part of a peace agreement between Minos and Aegeus, and how Theseus had set off for Crete under a black sail, promising Aegeus he'd return under a white sail if he was successful in killing the Minotaur, and how Ariadne, smitten with Theseus, had given him a ball of string to tie to the door of the labyrinth that housed the Minotaur, the labyrinth built at the behest of King Minos by none other than Daedalus, the finest craftsman the world had ever known, the labyrinth where Theseus eventually confronted and killed the Minotaur, rescued all fourteen Athenian youth in the bargain and led them safely back through the labyrinth with the help of Ariadne's thread and made his escape from Crete, taking Ariadne with him, but abandoning her later on the island of Naxos where she, scorned, put a curse on Theseus and caused him to forget to change his sail from black to white to proclaim his success to his father and, Aegeus, seeing the black sail, threw himself in despair off the cliffs into the sea that came to bear his name, after which relation and several more glasses of straight Scotch, Jason said goodnight and thank you and left and made his way along the corridor to a bathroom where he'd just finished taking a piss when he hit the floor, not blacking out entirely, but somehow remaining dimly aware of the strangers who found him minutes later and dragged him through the stark green corridors of the bunkhouse with the marks from his boots leaving twin trails on the dirty tiles, and held him clumsily against the wall like an ungainly roll of canvas as they knocked on George's door and, not receiving an answer, left Jason there, his knees buckling slowly to the floor, his mind whirling away and away in ever-widening circles until he dreamed he was an eagle diving from a great height headlong down into a gyre of unending blackness.

...

With the offer from Mitchell and Dorothy, Saul felt that his plans for a whole new future in St. John's were finally coming to fruition. But the elation was short-lived. He didn't even have time to register for night school before the letter arrived. The old man needed looking after and Anthony felt he'd done more than his share by staying at home with him all through the war. He'd gone ahead and booked passage to Canada secure in the knowledge that Saul would accept the responsibility now and come home.

Saul packed his things that day. What else could he do? It would be a family disgrace to have old Simon wither into his dotage in Birthlayn alone and neglected. There was no way to bring him to St. John's and even though Mitchell and Dorothy might suggest such a thing, Saul knew the impossibility of it.

Over a period of hours, step by unwilling step, Saul made one long last walk back out to the farm. He even refused a couple of rides, one in an automobile and another in a horse and gig, as if the added time spent walking would somehow stave off the inevitable. It was a hot day, even for September, and he sweaty and thirsty when he got there. He poured himself a drink of cold water in the main house, found no one about, so walked down to the country house by the pond and found Dorothy there, inside alone, cleaning out the wood stove with a spruce bough.

"Mitchell's mother showed me how to do it," she said. "I love how it makes the place smell, don't you? You should, since it's yours to live in now, for a while at least."

"I won't be living here," he said. "My father's not well. I'm needed at home to look after him. I have to leave right away."

She sat down at the table beside the cold stove and studied her hands and forearms blackened with soot.

"God," she said, and tossed the bough with its twigs all snapped and broken into the coal bucket. "Mitchell will be so disappointed. He's gone into town for supplies." She looked up at him. "When will you be back?"

All Saul could think was how beautiful she was and how much he was going to miss her.

"I don't know," he said. "He's a feisty old bugger, my old man; he could live on for years. So, I don't know if I'll ever ..."

"Don't, Saul. Don't say you'll never be back because that's just too sad. You'll be back. It's only a matter of time. Right?"

"That's right," he said, recalling Mitchell's favourite phrase. "It's only a matter of time."

He crossed to where a small drop leaf table with a ewer and basin on it stood beside the window. He poured some water into the basin.

"Here. You wash up now," he said.

She stepped between him and the table and started washing her arms and hands. He felt the awkwardness of it but stayed close, his behind against the cold stove, his crotch inches from her. She slipped the knotted bandana from her hair and dropped it on the table. A breeze gusted though the raised window and he watched goose bumps form on her exposed skin.

Once clean, she dipped her right hand into the ewer's open mouth and gathered her long dark hair into her left. He watched the silver droplets pool at her fingertips and fall one by one onto her bare neck. She lay the cooling hand there for a second, then the hair fell again, like a heartbeat, a handful of time. She sighed with relief, but stayed there with her head bent forward. Somehow, he knew that she was smiling and that made him take a step toward her.

His desire arrived in a flood and he was hard against her in seconds, faster even than he might have wished since there was no mistaking his passion now, no going back or apologizing for a false move. The fact of it was pressing into her. His heart stayed in his throat a long second or two until she pressed back. Then he leaned against the stove and took her weight with him. He pulled her dress up slowly, one handful at a time, the sharp intake of her breath urging him on.

She leaned harder into him, rotating against his groin. Still, he was reluctant to make the next move but then her hand reached back to reassure him, felt the strength of his desire beneath his trousers and fumbled with the buttons. He popped them open one by one. Then, so as not to have her the total instigator, he slipped her drawers down with his thumbs just far enough to leverage himself between the elastic band and the surprising wetness between her legs. He pushed into her, hesitantly, at first, until she leaned forward and he could watch himself disappear completely inside her.

Then she reached behind and placed her hand on his neck, pulled his head toward her, and simulated his thrusts into her with those of her hot wet tongue into his mouth. Before long, he shuddered to a climax. She stepped away to compose herself and he turned away to button up. He looked around in time to see her pick up the coal bucket and walk out the door.

He found her by the side of the pond minutes later.

"Tell Mitchell I'm sorry," he said. "Tell him I'll miss him."

"I will."

She was smoking a cigarette and looking thoughtfully across the water. The traces of her red lipstick on the filter risked inflaming his desire again until she flung the cigarette into the pond where it extinguished in a black hiss. They watched in silence as the glued paper came unstuck and shreds of tobacco slowly dispersed into the water.

"We'll miss you too, Saul," she said at last, and turned and walked away.

...

One September day after school Jasie Dade walked down the road to Johnnie Breen's house to see if Johnnie was interested in going jumping fences or searching for birds' nests. Instead, he found Johnnie glued to the television set in the living room.

"Hey, Johnnie, ya wanna go ..."

"Sssshhhhh!"

Johnnie was intent upon the TV screen where, of all things, a game of baseball was unfolding. "Bob Gibson has fourteen strikeouts," he said. "He might break the record."

Baseball.

Jasie had never given much thought to baseball. Sure, it was on television every now and again, and the rules were basically the same as the softball they played in the Groves, but he couldn't name a single player on any team and there weren't any teams from Canada. So why would he give a shit about baseball? Yet, Johnnie was acting like it was the Maple Leafs against the Canadians or something, so Jasie figured there must be something to it. He plopped himself into an armchair and in a short while got caught up in the excitement as he watched Bob Gibson, the pitcher for the St. Louis Cardinals, set a new record for the most strikeouts in a game, *and* win Game Five of the World Series to put the Cardinals ahead three to one. When it was all over Jasie had to admit that it was pretty exciting stuff.

"Next game is day after tomorrow," Johnnie said, as he led Jasie upstairs to forage for a while through his amazing comic book collection. "Get down here right after school and we'll watch."

"For sure," said Jasie, though now he was itching to get his hands on Johnnie's latest edition of the Two Gun Kid. The Two Gun Kid was the only cowboy comic book hero who had a secret identity, the only one who wore a mask the way "super" heroes like The Flash and Green Lantern did. This touch of mystery made him Jasie's favourite in the line of western comics.

Jasie watched the next two games at Johnnie's house, rooting for his newly-adopted favourite team, the St. Louis Cardinals, who looked like a sure thing to win until the Tigers battled back to tie the series three-all. Jasie was sure, though, that with Bob Gibson back on the mound in Game Seven the Cardinals would win it all.

Then he had an exciting idea. He would watch the big game at home. His father, who, Jasie had often noticed, had a certain admiration for Americans, would likely be impressed by his son's appreciation of the all-American game.

On the big day, Saul sat on the couch beside Jasie, taking a middling interest in the game, and smoking. Strangely, he offered no comment, not even when the game took its most spectacular turns. Mickey Lolich was on the mound for the Tigers and he and Bob Gibson fought a scoreless pitchers' duel until the Tigers broke out and scored three runs in the seventh inning. Then, when Lou Brock got thrown out stealing second base in the eighth, stalling a Cardinals' rally, Jasie grew uneasy for his team.

"Uh-oh," he said, "this doesn't look good." His tone was so casual that it actually startled him that he'd spoken to his father that way.

"What doesn't look good?" Saul replied, dryly.

"Lou Brock got thrown out stealing second."

"He got thrown out for stealing second?"

"No, he tried to steal ..."

"Is it against the rules to steal?"

"No, it's ..."

"Then why did they throw him out?"

Jasie realised, with a start of fear and embarrassment, that his father knew nothing about baseball. The man had been staring at the TV the whole time the way an illiterate person might stare into the pages of a book. Jasie mumbled something to mask his discomfort and they watched the rest of the game in silence.

That day the underdog Detroit Tigers won the World Series, and little Jasie Dade realised that he probably knew more about the Two Gun Kid than he did about his own father. He felt like he'd been sitting on the couch beside a complete stranger. And he dared not speculate on the even darker possibility that, after all the years of the family watching it together on television, his father didn't understand the rules of hockey either.

Time was passing in North City and Virgil's advice about following Ariadne's thread wasn't really paying off for Jason. There didn't seem to be a thread, any thread, leading anywhere, or else there were so many threads he didn't know which to follow; nor could he recognize any pattern or sign that might lead him from where he was, as Virgil had so neatly put it, to where he needed to be. He was lost. He'd been in North City for nearly a month doing whatever the next thing was and not getting anywhere. In the meantime, the days were getting shorter and the nights colder. He knew it would soon get much, much colder and he was annoyed at the idea of having to spend money on winter clothes. He usually wandered around town all day, smoked dope in various bunkhouse rooms, continued to drink every night at The Pit, and remained constantly on the lookout for any presentiment of The Man. He was even beginning to think it was time to search elsewhere, but he had no idea how to get out of North City. He'd already gone back twice to ask George for more money and dreaded the prospect of asking him for airfare.

One night he went for a long walk and eventually, partially in an effort to get in out of the cold, partially following his nose, he walked in the front entrance of the local hospital and inconspicuously locked himself in a public washroom off the main lobby. He let his long black coat slip from his shoulders and stared intensely at his reflection in the mirror. Then he undressed to the waist, plugged the washbasin and let the tap water run icy cold. When the basin filled he put his head under the water until it ached. After dousing himself like this several times, he dried his hair with his undershirt and studied himself again in the mirror. He leaned into his reflection until his nose was pressed right up against the glass. On an impulse, he closed his eyes and let his head fall carefully to the right, then, ever so slowly, he opened his right eye. It filled his vision like a glittering diamond. Then he let his head fall carefully to the left, his eyelash brushed the glass and there was the open left eye, vastly different from the right somehow, vulnerable, gentle and sad.

A man must use both eyes to see the world. The right eye is reason and strength, the left is compassion. This discovery, he decided, was the secret purpose of his walk. He took some small comfort from that, put his damp shirt back on, turned off the light, and made a bed for himself on the impeccably polished linoleum.

...

One Friday afternoon in late September Jasie Dade stood on the front steps of his house studying his reflection in the kitchen window. The glass was darkened in the failing light, but Jasie could plainly see that his hair, despite his best efforts, was way too short. He had combed the hair down his forehead and feathered it over his ears as best he could to look like one of the Beatles, but it wasn't working. It was his last year at Princeton Junior High and with the prospect of high school on the horizon, hair, especially long hair, was becoming important. He was learning to be cool and he wanted to make a good impression at the school dance that night.

Then he heard a tap-tap-tapping from inside. He peered into the dark glass and saw that his father had been watching him the whole time. A finger beckoned.

Jasie passed uneasily through the porch and into the kitchen.

Saul had set a chair in the middle of the floor. He stood behind it with a white sheet thrown over his arm and a pair of electric clippers in his hand. As far as Jasie was concerned, it might as well have been a hood and a hangman's noose.

"Sit down," Saul said, "and I'll give you a trim before the dance."

And so the awful business began.

Saul always set out with good intentions, mindful of past mistakes as he went gingerly about the work: a nip here, another there, side to side and back again, the occasional sortie down to the nape to get it all even, but soon enough the electric clippers had, once again, somehow gotten beyond his control. After thirty wordless minutes that thin grey rail of baldness that was the bowl-on-the-head haircut had somehow, despite his best efforts, magically appeared on his son's head.

Saul looked down to see the hair lying in dark clumps on the floor. He guiltily swept it up and threw it in the stove. "That'll do ya," he said, and pulled the sheet off with a flourish. It was false bravado; he knew he'd gone too far. He stared down dismally at what could only be described as an appalling haircut. If he *had* placed a bowl on the young fellow's head and made one deep cut along its edge he could have achieved more or less the same result in under five seconds.

But it was too late to do anything about it now.

Jasie did not go to the bathroom to check his look, but went quietly to his room, dressed for the dance and reappeared with a heavy woollen cap on his head. When the boy asked for his dollar to get into the dance, Saul penitently handed over a second one. The boy stared down at twice the price of a *real* haircut at the barbershop in Princeton and then up at his father with an expression so sad it might have borne witness to a thousand crucifixions. And Saul suddenly understood how many such dollars the boy would gladly have given just to have the hair burning and stinking in the stove back on his head again.

A short time later Saul sat at the kitchen table watching his boy wend his way up the road and he pondered this idea he'd heard talked about on television, that the times they were a-changing. At the age of fifteen Saul Dade had been a veteran of the lumber camps, he'd slept on a bed of boughs, eaten nothing but beans three time a day, and had his body invaded by lice. Once he'd barely escaped being eaten by a bear. So he found it difficult to credit a boy of nearly fourteen years being undone by a bad haircut.

But there it was.

When it came to cutting hair, Saul was merely the slave of tradition. When he'd been a boy his own father had done the barbering for the family as a way to save a few dollars. But Saul had never counted on this thing known as "being cool." Oh, in his day a man could be suave or debonair, in the manner of Ronald Coleman, or dashing like Errol Flynn, but this "being cool" was another thing altogether. Saul couldn't make head nor tail of it, except to be fairly certain that, whatever it was, it had absolutely nothing to do with actually being a man.

Still, something about that evening sitting at the table watching his downcast son make his reluctant way up the road finally convinced Saul Dade to reach a little deeper into his own pockets and hang up his clippers for good.

October

When he got to high school, Jason Dade was still "Jasie" to an older generation in Birthlayn but the teachers at Princeton High consistently called him Jason and the practice was gradually catching on among his peers. He liked the grown-up feeling it gave him.

The high school building itself was a one-floor structure that lay on the Great Beach in Princeton in the perfect formation of a cross. In one arm of the crossbeam the nuns taught the girls and in the other the Christian Brothers taught the boys. The gymnasium, where both sexes gathered warily during lunch and recess, formed the stout upright of the cross, and the administrative offices were lodged, appropriately, in the head. Sitting in his classroom on the first day of school Jason fancifully imagined that his desk was placed exactly where one of the nails might pierce the hand of an imaginary giant crucifix lying supine on the school building. He imagined there was a pretty girl in a corresponding desk seated somewhere on the other side. *Would he meet her perhaps?*

The boys sat in neat rows cautiously looking around at one another wearing their white shirts and jackets and neckties. They'd come from smaller high schools in the area, now closed to supply this larger "regional" one. Jason caught the eye of Johnnie Breen, the only other boy from Birthlayn in his Grade Nine class. Very soon, basketball would bring the two boys together, daily trudging the long road back to Birthlayn after practices, fall, winter, and spring, in all weathers. Johnnie was in the middle of a growth spurt that would eventually guarantee him a place as the starting centre. Jason was learning fast, too, and would eventually play right guard.

The homeroom teacher, Brother Bryce, was one of a new breed of hip young religious who sang and played acoustic guitar in English class. He would be the one to show Jason that song lyrics could actually *mean* things. In songs like "The Times They Are A-Changin'" and "Blowin' in the Wind", Brother Bryce sang to them about a world in need of their attention and concern, while in "Mrs. Robinson" and "Eleanor Rigby", he revealed people's tragic inner lives. Yes, a new world of song was opening up to the boy raised on "Sixteen Tons." He perked up when Brother Bryce told them that "Puff the Magic Dragon" (puff-the-magic drag-in) by Peter, Paul, and Mary was really about a mysterious substance called marijuana that was being smoked, mostly in the United States, by people called hippies.

One day, around the second week of October, the boys leapt to their feet when the classroom door opened and the principal, Brother Batterson, walked in. Brother had come to give the first year boys what was to become his annual lecture on the evils of the flesh — most particularly, their own.

"A *good* boy ..." Brother Batterson was soon proclaiming, his fist in a clench and his tongue poking defiantly into his cheek as he paused for emphasis, "does not take his *flesh* into his hands." This horrifying speech instantly brought Jason to a considerable state of remorse over certain things that he was doing in secret in the bathroom at home, and he immediately formed a silent resolution to resist all future temptations of that kind. And for some mysterious reason the restraint came surprisingly easy; Jason didn't put his hands on himself once during the three years of high school that followed.

It turned out his old primary school teacher Miss Crockwell had become the new librarian at Princeton High. She would continue to be impressed with the boy Jason and his reading choices. She watched as his literary tastes matured, seeking out the likes of Steinbeck's *Of Mice and Men* or Bronte's *Wuthering Heights*, though she observed he did retain a fondness for quick reads like *The Hardy Boys* or, his new favourite, the *Chip Hilton Sports Stories*. Chip Hilton was the master of every sport and the hero of every tournament, usually staging impressive comebacks against tremendous odds. Miss Crockwell marvelled whenever Jason borrowed one of the hardcover books in the series and brought it back read the next day.

But it was the short sharp shock of *Of Mice and Men* that marked the end of Jason's reading at home from his Aunt Agnes's encyclopedia. He'd read every entry in every volume from A-Z twice through, but when he closed Steinbeck's novel and spent the next two days brooding about it, he knew it was time to turn the encyclopedia over to his sister Sarah. Soon, he noticed, she was reading an entry or two every night before bedtime, just as he used to when he was little Jasie Dade instead of a growing up boy who went to high school, a boy eager to read books that didn't just tell him about things, but actually held stories with the power to inspire or even break his young heart in two.

...

If Jason had thought about it much at all — which he hadn't — he would have realised that there wasn't very much to like about his newest North City companion, a man nick-named Lenin (because of his resemblance to the communist revolutionary) who rarely smiled, often complained, and frequently spoke ill of others. In his room, Lenin would hide his face behind a thick paperback for hours at a time, displaying a concentration seemingly impervious to the effects of Jason's biggest four-paper joints. They often spent hours together there, barely talking, Jason slouched against a wall on the floor, thinking, or reading something from Lenin's paperback collection. When they did speak, it could be on any subject except, pointedly, whatever it was Lenin did at the mine. There was an unspoken understanding that Jason could crash in Lenin's room as long as there was something to smoke on offer. And because of what he detected to be a mysterious, though somewhat malevolent, glint in Lenin's eye, Jason entertained the notion that, in some way yet to be revealed, this fellow would be important to his master plan.

There were better books in Lenin's room than in George's, the literary remnants of Lenin's two years at university, mostly slim volumes from Political Science and English courses. One that immediately caught Jason's eye was *The Collected Works of T.S. Eliot*, the small green hardcover version that had gone into endless reprints, the one he'd owned himself as part of the first-year course he'd barely attended and which was now at home in Birthlayn buried in the cardboard box of meagre possessions that had somehow survived his time in St. John's. He had vague recollections of one lecture he *had* attended as he opened the Eliot at random and read:

Time present and time past
Are both perhaps present in time future
And time future contained in time past...

"Hey."

It was Lenin, staring at him over his current paperback, the massive *Atlas Shrugged.*

"You want to go to The Pit?"

"Sure."

A short while later they were standing at the bar amid a cluster of patrons when Lenin put on a little show of interrogating Jason:

"Tell me something, Jason," he said, "what're you doin' here in North City?"

"I'm waiting."

"Yes, b'y! What are ya waitin' for then?"

"I'm waiting to see what happens next."

"Okay ... but what brought you here in the first place?"

"Nothing *brought* me here. I came here because I had to."

"Yeah. Me too. I had to come for the money."

"I didn't come for the money."

"That's right, you're not workin', are ya?"

"Work is not a priority at the moment."

"Well now."

The exchange was attracting attention and people quietened down to listen.

"So how long you gonna stay here then?"

"As long as it takes."

"As long as *what* takes?"

"Waiting."

"For the next thing?"

"Right."

Lenin played openly to his audience now.

"And has it happened yet? This *thing*."

"It's happening right now, actually. It's always happening."

"How will you know when it's over, then?"

"Because it will be."

"Over?"

"Yes."

"*When* though?"

"When it is."

"*But how will you know when it is?*"

"Because it will be."

"Over?"

"Yes."

Lenin laughed and took a small bow.

"Well, b'ys," Lenin said, grinning, "*I* can't get a lick of sense out of him. Perhaps one of you would like to have a crack at 'im?"

"Why don't *you* get a fuckin' life?" someone called from a table.

"Leave the young fella alone!"

"There's no need for that shit, man."

"Arsehole."

And everyone went back to what they were doing before Lenin spoke. Jason wasn't surprised that people came to his defence. He knew that most people could easily understand what he was doing and that, yes, Lenin *was* being an arsehole.

Lenin ordered a double whiskey, slammed it back, and announced he was going back to his room. Though he didn't care for the shenanigans Jason went along anyway, deciding this would be his last night crashing there. When they got to the room, Lenin immediately went down the hall to take a shower. Alone in the room, Jason prepared a thick spliff, then took a blanket and pillow from the closet and lay down on the floor. Lenin came back and they smoked the doobie, Lenin admiring himself in the full-length mirror on the door, drying and fussing with his hair before he finally took off his bathrobe, flicked off the wall switch with a karate kick and hopped into bed. Jason's eyes adjusted to the light of the gibbous moon that had hung on their shoulders during the cold walk home. Then he turned his face toward the baseboard heater and tried to sleep.

It had been another long concerning day with no signs.

He was drifting off to sleep when he heard the click of the bedside lamp. He didn't react since Lenin often read in bed.

But then he heard:

"Hey, Jason?"

"Yeah?"

"Will you do something for me?"

"If I can. Sure."

"Just take a look at this, will ya?"

Jason turned to see that Lenin had pushed the blankets down and filched his erect cock out of his briefs. He was holding it at the base, waving it about like a baton.

"Why don't you suck that off for me right now?"

Jason jumped to his feet, pulled on his boots, grabbed his coat and headed out the door. He walked the corridors until he came to a four-way intersection. Looking around he saw Lenin, in jeans, shirtless and barefoot, hurrying toward him. Jason spread his arms wide and turned himself to face each corridor in turn, as if they were the cardinal points of the compass, then launched himself into the air, backwards, floating free and groundless for a second or two until he landed heavily on his back with a loud bang smack dab in the middle of the intersection, arms and legs akimbo as if he'd just made a snow angel.

Then he started screaming at the top of his lungs.

...

Despite the mysterious and prophetic statements of the tattooed man, Saul Dade never once allowed himself to seriously entertain the possibility of some kind of buried treasure in Birthlayn. In fact, it had occurred to him soon after that heady night of drinking and smoking in Ballater that the Russian Petro might have found a perverse enjoyment in befuddling drunken sailors and sending them on empty quests. He'd grown suspicious, too, about what might have been in that Turkish cigarette. His fellow sailors had told him that things more exotic (and intoxicating) than tobacco were commonly smoked in Turkey.

He also toyed with the idea that Petro was simply touched in the head.

But then again ... it was hard not to give the prediction at least some credence, especially since there actually *was* an immense boulder on the Downs of the kind that Petro had described. That night in the bar Saul had instantly remembered seeing, as a boy through the kitchen window of the house, a massive grey stone slouched and solemn in an open meadow. The years since had seen the woods encroach upon it, but Saul had never forgotten it was there. As a boy he'd been struck by the way rainwater pooled in the shallow bowl of its surface and he'd occasionally released live trout there to watch them swim in a confined space. The stone had never been named and it struck him as odd that no one in Birthlayn besides himself, apparently, had ever taken particular notice of such a large boulder sitting all by itself in the landscape. It also occurred to him that he was in sole possession of this curious wisdom since Benjamin Breen had rather stupidly slept through the entire Thunder Stone conversation and missed out on the chance to capitalise on any possible revelation.

...

Once Jason Dade got to high school he found that report card night was always easier if his father was working up north and Mother was the one who went instead to hear what the teachers had to say. A good report card got a smile and a pat on the back from her, a poor one earned a little chastisement, maybe a warning or two, and ten minutes later everyone went back to homework or TV.

It was different when the old man was home, as he was on the October night Jason was copying out the final draft of his research paper on communism, sitting at the kitchen table with a brand new ballpoint pen, scribing his words carefully onto impeccably clean loose leaf, twice underlining the rubric COMMUNISM at the top of each page, carefully marking the page numbers in the exact same spot two lines from the bottom. He'd picked COMMUNISM out of a hatful of topics passed around in social studies three weeks earlier and had since researched the subject in the Princeton library. His thorough research, mature writing style, accurate citations, and overall neatness and attention to detail would likely, once again, earn him the "A" he usually got for such work.

His father had gone a couple of hours earlier to see the teachers about report cards. For the fourth or fifth time George came out of his room, looked up at the clock, sighed, went back in and closed the door. Sarah and Jason always did their homework at the kitchen table, but it had been decided that George would do better if he studied alone in his room. (Jason suspected he spent a lot of time daydreaming in there instead.) George struggled in school generally and had already failed Grade Seven, the difficult transition year from Birthlayn to Princeton — Jason had not only passed that year but surprised himself by coming first in his class to boot — but if George passed his Grade Eleven this year he would be done with school, and Saul seemed to be looking forward to that very much indeed. With George's graduation in sight, Saul's speeches about "not keeping him after high school" had become louder and more frequent around the house.

It was almost nine o'clock when a pair of headlights finally stopped outside instead of disappearing in a swoosh down the road. Jason peered through the curtain and saw the dome light of a taxi. Father was home. There was a muffled exchange with the driver, the slam of the car door, the crunch of footsteps on gravel, then a lighter tread on the wooden steps, an ominous rustling about in the porch for the light string and, at last, his father's head popped inside the kitchen door. His eyeglasses steamed up immediately in the rush of heat. This put a big silly grin on his father's face.

The sour smell of beer and tobacco drifted to Jason's nostrils. Saul removed his hat and coat and hung them in the little recess by the door. Jason was alone in the kitchen at the time and managed to say "Hello, Father," though he wasn't at all sure if total silence might not be the safer course. His mother, he knew, was already too angry to come out of the living room.

Saul walked unsteadily across the kitchen and hugged Jason to him. Jason used to love the smell of beer, but that smell now, mingled with tobacco and the icy scrape of his father's cheek, he found deeply unsettling.

"You're a good boy," his father said quietly. "You're a very good boy."

Jason tried to imagine what the teachers might have said to make his father say that.

George chose that exact moment to put on a brave face and walk into the kitchen.

Saul, at the sight of him, flew into a towering rage.

"You're no good!" he howled, and went for him. George, half expecting it, bolted back to the room and locked the door.

Saul pounded on the door with his fist, repeating over and over, "You've got to get out of here, do you understand me, get out of here, you've got to get out of this fucking place ..." until, white and trembling, he slumped into the rocking chair beneath the Bless Our House cardboard crucifix. Jason wondered what the teachers could possibly have said about George to make his father act this way. He looked down at his own hands and saw them white and trembling. But he willed them to arrange his pages and attach a paper clip to the impeccably completed assignment.

...

George Dade has hardly seen Jason since October came in. He has no idea where his brother has been sleeping these days either. It seems the whole bunkhouse has more or less adopted him. One reason is that Jason always has a ready supply of hash — George has no idea where he's getting it, only that it's being purchased with *his* money — and this, no doubt, opens doors to rooms where Jason can crash. In any case, he knows Jason has this way of taking up easily with strangers, treating them like instant collaborators in some grand and secret enterprise. Trouble is, George really doesn't know most of these people. Virgil, for example, he knows only as a chronic alcoholic who makes periodic trips to detox in St. John's and who apparently keeps whole cases of whiskey in his room.

George recalls the night he came home from work and found Jason, after an evening with Virgil, slumped unconscious against the door with vomit gurgling in his throat. Another half an hour and the kid might have choked to death. What the hell business did Virgil have drinking a seventeen-year-old boy into oblivion like that?

Lately, Jason has been hanging around with this guy everyone calls Lenin. They call him that because he looks like that commie in the history books. Beady black eyes. Little goatee. George doesn't like him. Hardly ever pays for a drink at The Pit, instead sneaks to the bathroom or heads home when it's his turn to buy a round. Lenin likes his draw too, and that's his interest in Jason, right there. Free dope. Plain and simple.

George gets up and goes to the window to see the dazzling dome of the night sky. He presses his hand to the wall and feels the arctic air outside waging war with the baseboard heaters, trying to invade his space and turn the entire building into a block of ice. It's cold enough out there to freeze a man solid in a few hours.

He reads for a bit and has just turned out his bedside lamp when the scream makes him sit bolt upright in bed. *Jason.* It came from upstairs. He jumps out of bed, pulls on his jeans and is in the hallway in seconds, shirtless, bare feet slapping on the gritty linoleum.

What the hell has my crazy brother gotten himself into now?

It turned out that Saul's father, old Simon, though infirm, was more crotchety and disagreeable than ever. Saul found little joy or satisfaction in finding himself alone in the house with the old man and after only a few days of it he employed Ana Cruet, a woman of ancient French extraction who lived nearby, to come by twice weekly to do the housekeeping and give Saul a much needed break.

Eventually, Saul decided it *would* be a good idea to at least undertake the walk to the Downs to explore the stone which, despite his best efforts not to think about it, had been playing on his mind since his arrival back in Birthlayn.

One nagging question concerned what time of day to take the walk; another was whether or not to take a shovel. No one had gardened on the Downs for years, so to be seen heading over there with a shovel, especially toward evenfall when it would be safest to do some digging undetected, would definitely invite awkward questions, and since he preferred to keep the whole matter of the treasure a secret, especially since there was very likely nothing to it, he was for a number of weeks paralysed by indecision.

October nights brought the realisation that the ground would soon be frozen and he decided to make his move. He waited for a day when Ana was looking after old Simon and asked if she would mind staying into the evening. This would allow him to leave the house in fading daylight, work well enough under a clear night sky, then return home under a reasonable cover of darkness. Feeling that every eye in Birthlayn was on him, he took the shovel in hand and walked all the way round the Front Pond. He exchanged brief pleasantries with a couple of women who seemed to take scant notice of him as they busied themselves in their yards. He quickened his pace on the footbridge between the two ponds and hurried up the rocky lane to be, at last, safely out of view under the trees.

He was a little disoriented at first by the encroaching darkness and the changes time had wrought in once familiar terrain. He tripped over a root and gave his shin a nasty smack with the blade of the shovel. He didn't check but felt sure that it was bleeding. He partially got his bearings from lights coming on in the houses across the pond, headed toward them and lucked upon the stone right in the middle of a droke, its dark presence surrounded by a seemingly magic circle of maturing spruce and fir trees.

In the sky the stars were appearing slowly, a gibbous moon hung low in the west. Saul reckoned that in half an hour there would ample light to work by. He leaned his shovel against the cool stone and rolled a cigarette. Soon, only the most discerning eye could see the red ember of his cigarette arcing back and forth in the dark.

...

It was the tournament's championship game. The score was 42-40 and Jason's team was behind with 12 seconds left on the clock. The ball was put inbounds to Jason. A quick glance at the clock and he started dribbling down court, weighing his options as the meagre seconds ticked away. His first instinct — no, it was more than an instinct; it was a strong and immediate impulse — was to cross the centreline, stop, focus-focus-focus, and unleash one of those long arcing set shots that he'd spent so many hours perfecting on weekends and after school.

Ten seconds.

To take that shot would be a huge risk, for if he missed and the rebound went awry they would almost certainly lose the game, but on the other hand, no one was expecting him to do that, so no opposing player would be near enough to even distract him, let alone block the shot; besides that, in his mind's eye he saw the ball arcing through the air in an eerie awestruck silence, then swish through the hoop to thunderous applause, he saw the gym floor flooded with elated students, and himself, pawed and tousled, clutched in the sweaty embrace of exhausted and ecstatic teammates.

Eight seconds.

But more than that, it was a *feeling* he had inside, a feeling that filtered through the pandemonium around him, that called to mind those boyhood days in Birthlayn when he roamed the meadows and woods on imaginary horses, ready to accomplish brave deeds, to astonish and amaze whenever occasion allowed.

Six seconds.

He crossed the centreline and, as expected, the opposing players crouched, arms aloft, in a zone defence formation and, instead of moving forward to harass him, they waited for him to pass or attempt a futile drive through the middle. No one was expecting him to shoot.

Five seconds.

It was now or never.

Four seconds.

It was never. The opposing guards, sensing trouble, had moved in on him. So Jason drove straight down the middle for the layup and hopefully a foul. If he missed the layup he'd get two foul shots and, if he made them, send the game into overtime. If he scored on the layup, his trip to the foul line could win the game. He'd scored two points at the foul line already and he had that same strong feeling that he could do it again.

Then, out of the corner of his eye, he saw Johnnie Breen, left unguarded when the opposing players had suddenly converged on Jason.

Three seconds.

Johnnie was a short jump shot from the basket and Jason decided to let him be the one to make or break it.

Two seconds.

He bounced the pass and Johnnie, caught off guard, scooped it up and took the shot.

One second.

The shot was short. An air ball. Jason had a fleeting image of himself leaping to the ball mid-flight and tipping it into the basket, but the opposing centre snatched it fiercely away and, then, at last, it was over.

"You should've gone for the layup," Johnnie said to him later, resentment in his voice, before parting after their long silent walk back home. And that was not entirely fair of Johnnie — after all, Jason had handed him a pretty easy shot — but Jason knew it was the simple truth, that the moment had properly belonged to him, and that to hand it off to another at the last second amounted to a cowardly refusal of what he was being called upon to do. But Johnnie was wrong about one thing. It wasn't the layup. It was the long shot that had marked the moment of truth, and it was the long shot that would be forever untaken, and it was the long shot that Jason thought about so much in the weeks and months that followed, asking himself over and over why he hadn't taken that shot when the voice inside him had said so clearly that he should and he somehow knew in his heart that he would have made it good if only, if only, if only, if only he had.

...

George appeared at the corridor intersection to find Jason lying supine on the filthy linoleum while Lenin, a few feet away, talked to him in hushed tones.

Then Jason screamed again, the sound ripping through the empty hallways, leaving George shaken by the depth and duration of it.

"What the fuck is going on here?"

He stepped into the intersection with the casual air of a rodeo rider. He saw that he and the fucker in the goatee were both barefoot and shirtless, clad only in jeans.

"None of your fucking business," the fucker replied.

George took another step forward.

"You looking for a smack in the mouth?" he said. His thumbs fell from the belt loops and his fists dropped easily to his sides. Lenin stood back, broadened his stance and raised his arms in what looked like some phony fucking martial arts thing that would likely collapse in seconds under the furious frontal assault that George was seconds from unleashing. George didn't have abs like this guy, and certainly didn't know any fancy-ass Kabuki bullshit when it came to fighting, but he'd been in dust-ups with men big and tough enough to eat this little fucker alive. On top of that, George packed a wallop in his right fist that had flattened a lot of those men, and he wanted nothing more right then than to add some of Lenin's blood to the road salt and ore dust staining the grimy floor.

He wasn't surprised when Lenin's gaze faltered and the little commie turned his back and retreated to his room.

Jason's voice rose eerily from the floor.

"Just leave me here, Georgie. Okay? I'll be fine. I just want to lie here for a little while and figure things out. Okay?"

And George knew enough by then to just walk away and let him be.

...

It wasn't long before Saul Dade began to see the folly in this strange night work he'd undertaken. For one thing, though the soil wasn't as rocky and impenetrable as untilled soil might be elsewhere in Birthlayn, the breaking of two fallow generations of sod clearly called for a gruff in addition to the sharp-pointed shovel he'd brought along. But he set to work with a will, his idea being to dig a trench about two feet deep and wide around the perimeter of the stone, all the while waiting for the telltale clink of something that might be a treasure. He reassured himself that there were plenty of old stories about pirate treasure buried and abandoned in coves up and down the shore. So why not here? And particularly, why not beside what had once been such a conspicuous landmark as this lesser thunder stone?

He also realised that his plan would involve making at least a second trip to the Downs at night, that is, unless he intended to spend this entire night digging. He looked at his watch. It was six o'clock. He decided he would have to be back to the house by ten, the latest he could reasonably expect Ana to stay on with the old man. He would have to walk her home and to do so any later than that would be to invite unwelcome speculations of another kind.

A couple of hours later he checked his watch again. His back was aching, his injured shin was wailing, his hands were blistering, but a nice trail of black earth lay excavated behind him along one side of the stone. The physical exertions were hard enough, but more difficult was the mental struggle of continually fending off the idea that he was being ridiculous. The dread that he might be discovered in this foolish quest, now that he was at last about it, mortified him more than he'd imagined it could. What would people think when they saw this broken ground? Would they ever figure out who'd done it and why? He imagined the strange and perhaps lurid stories that would arise in superstitious minds. Could he ever own up to being the one responsible, and, if so, what reason would he give? Could he tell the truth? Would it really be thought weak and ridiculous to have been susceptible to the promise of treasure from so strange and exotic a source?

I tell you, Saul Dade, in the place of this stone there is a treasure and it will help you obtain everything you seek.

What he was seeking, he realised, was a way to get out of Birthlayn, a way to have a life for himself in the city, a life that included Mitch and Dorothy, though all that might be lost to him now in any case because of what had happened between himself and Dorothy, a thing, try as he might, that he simply couldn't bring himself to regret. Yet a life, any life of that order, with or without them, would require money that he didn't have and would likely never have and that was why he was there, risking being made a laughing stock in this place he was more or less being forced to once again make his home.

An hour later, he decided to smoke one last cigarette and head back to the house. The old man would be in bed by now and it would be pleasant enough to end the day walking Ana up the road. She was good with the old bastard, surprisingly so, and Saul felt favourably disposed to her. The woman was still single in her thirties because of, Saul could only presume, an absurd generations-old prejudice in Birthlayn against people of French extraction. Yet another reason to take a dim view of the place.

He pinched tobacco from his pack and parsed it along a rolling paper. With one hand he tucked and rolled the paper into a neat white cylinder, licked it, struck a match, and raised it toward his face. That's when he heard a cough somewhere off to his left in the dark and then, as if it had been some sort of signal, a match flared off to the right, then another to his left, and another, and another, and then he heard laughter, and the mocking sound of his name and he grabbed his shovel and ran.

He almost immediately regretted the retreat, but decided it was too late, once he'd taken flight, to turn and face them. Besides, they probably would have stayed in hiding, taunting him through the dark, and the thought of enduring that was unbearable. Saul wasn't even sure who was there, but as he fled he imagined a day shortly after his departure from the Ballater logging camp, the men lying on the grass drinking their switchel and smoking cigarettes as Benjamin Breen, whose deception in all of this was unforgivable, regaled them with the story of how Saul was being sent on some foolish treasure hunt by a tattooed man who owned the local pub. He imagined the conspiracy taking shape against him as soon as he'd returned and he also couldn't help but imagine, as well, the complicity of the two women in the yard who'd seen him pass by on his way to the Downs with the shovel.

He doubted, however, that Ana Cruet was involved since she had always been exactly what he was about to become, an outcast.

With no way to save face Saul strode through the night, shovel in hand, swearing bitterly, all the way back to the house, that he would never speak to another soul of the Thunder Stone or that night in Ballater again.

...

It was Friday, the last weekend in October, eight weeks after Jason Dade had left home for university and so far he'd managed not to return to Birthlayn even once. This was all part of a deep commitment he felt — especially as a young fellow now living away from home with a set of keys to his own room — to the idea of growing up and changing. When he'd filled out the application for university some months back, he'd even taken the daring step of falsifying his date of birth. This, at registration, had provided him with a foolproof photo ID — Student # 6-7183294-5 — that said he would be turning twenty-one, the legal drinking age, instead of seventeen in November. It was a scheme he'd learned about in Princeton, designed to give underage students like himself unfettered access to the St. John's bars, but it had the added benefit of making it appear to some at least that he was older than he actually was.

He was staying away from Birthlayn and Princeton as long as possible so that everyone would see the great change in him when he finally did reappear. He wasn't sure exactly what the change would be though his sense of it was somehow tied to the idea that his hair would be much longer.

On this particular Friday night a bunch of heads he'd gotten to know had invited themselves to his room so everybody could get stoned before going to the concert at the Student Centre. "I Want You/She's So Heavy" was grinding out of the record player someone had brought along and set up on his desk. The twin beds in the room had been dismantled so that everyone could sit on mattresses on the floor while the chillums of hash were being passed around. Jason himself had had several large tokes. Though concerned about the noise emanating from his room, he did not want to be the one suggesting they keep it down. He was slumped on the floor against the room door when he heard the timorous knock.

He stood up to answer, but was arrested by his reflection in the full-length mirror on the door. His hair, parted in the middle and combed as much as possible over his ears, still looked strained and unnatural. He had a long way to go before being considered cool, but he was doing his best and learning fast. He could take some comfort in his khaki army jacket, blue jeans, and yellow truckin' boots — perfectly acceptable gear for a "head" to be wearing. He could roll a spliff or a joint with the best of them now and his fingers were respectably burnt and stained from smoking them down to the nub. Behind him in the mirror he saw Murray Roach, who'd brought the hash, neatly tuck his long tresses behind each ear. It was a gesture Jason coveted intensely.

The knock became a little more insistent. Jason opened the door a crack and saw Brendan Spurrell, another first year from down the hall, standing anxiously in the corridor, shifting his weight from one foot to the other as if disguising the fact that he needed to go to the bathroom. Poor Brendan had actually tried to impress Jason during their first week on campus by smoking a pipe ... a pipe full of *tobacco*, for Christ's sake — and bragging that he was going to major in philosophy.

Jason stuck his head out and squinted.

"What is it, Brendan?"

"There's a phone call for you," Brendan said, looking at the floor, trying to appear incurious about what was going on in the room.

"For me?"

"Yes, for you. Payphone downstairs off the main lobby."

"Okay. Thanks."

Jason watched Brendan toddle off down the corridor, then turned into the room to tell everyone he was leaving. But no one was paying the slightest bit of attention, so he slipped out.

The corridor was empty and all the room doors were closed, as they perennially seemed to be. His yellow trucking boots squeaked on the polished linoleum as he crossed his own floor, went down two flights of stairs and crossed the ground floor back to the phone booth off the main lobby. Still not a soul in sight. The door was ajar, and the receiver hung suspended at the end of a thick black wire. Jason picked it up and put it to his ear.

"Hello?" he said.

"When are you coming home?"

Jason experienced a profound sense of the words actually pushing their way through miles and miles of cramped black wire, working their way to him over the cold distance of woods and bogs and marshes that lay along the pole lines between St. John's and Birthlayn. He recognized his father's voice not so much by the sound of it as by the sudden image of Saul holding the handset of the phone in that delicate way he had, as if it was an eggshell, or a bomb that might explode at any second. Saul handled the new remote control in much the same way, pointing it imperiously at the television as if it had the power to make things vanish or explode instead of just switch on or off.

"When are you coming home?" the voice called again.

And that's when Jason started to cry. He couldn't even remember the last time he'd cried; a long time ago, in childhood, over some deprivation, humiliation, rejection, or physical injury — crying isn't much of a mystery when you're a child — but there, in the phone booth with his chest suddenly heaving with emotion and his eyes overflowing with tears Jason became a little frightened for himself. He'd only been away from home for a couple of months. What was the big deal?

If his father knew he was crying, there was no indication of it. Jason did his best to keep his voice free of emotion and blurted out a promise to come home the very next weekend.

"Make sure, now," his father said. "Your mother wants to see you." And Jason suddenly remembered being nursed through a childhood flu by his father: lying on a daybed in the kitchen, drifting feverishly in and out of sleep, Vicks VapoRub on a flannel cloth being applied to his chest; his father's calming words and patient hands.

They said goodbye and hung up. Maybe, Jason thought as he pulled himself together, he'd pushed things too far. Maybe he should have gone home, after all. He was beginning to see that change took time, and that he'd vastly underestimated the growth rate of human hair. He saw now that it would be six months at least before it would be anywhere near the length he needed it to be and he simply couldn't wait that long to go home.

He made his way back through the empty corridors, a sense of guilt and dread descending upon him about what his father would think if he knew what was going on in his absent son's room. Then he was seized by an idea. He got to the room, flicked on the light, and said, "My father's downstairs and he's coming up here in a minute."

It was amazing to watch how quickly they all scrambled out of there.

But they'd be back. Jason felt the rush of his absent father's power ebbing as he sat at his desk and wondered what to do. Hardly anyone from Princeton, and no one else from Birthlayn, not even Johnnie Breen, had come to university with him and, on top of that the Housing Office, for some unknown reason, hadn't supplied him with a roommate, which largely explained why his room had so easily become a hangout for his newest acquaintances. But mainly this was because Jason had a hard time saying no and, especially with no one there he could talk to about it, it was unlikely he was going to learn how anytime soon.

...

Jason has locked himself in the same North City hospital washroom where a few weeks ago he did his exploration of the eyes. Now he's stripped to the waist and staring profoundly into the mirror. Three months in this horrid little town and still no clue where he's going or what he's supposed to do next. There are no signs. An hour ago he turned on the hot water, provoking a whine of protest from somewhere deep within the building's bowels, and has watched as the room slowly fills with steam.

The mirror has become blurry and indistinct, drops of condensation slide madly down the glass. His refection looks covered with tears, but he's not crying. Instead, the beaded drops invite him to playfully write his name on the glass, the way he often did on slippery, dew-covered surfaces as a child.

He watches his hand rise from his side and reach toward the glass.

...

Later that night, after he'd walked Ana home, Saul Dade stood alone at the window staring out at the black waters of the pond, listening irritably to the old man snoring away upstairs. No hope of treasure on the Downs now; only rock-hard proof of his childish self-delusions lay there in the darkness, enclosed by solemn trees. It seemed everyone in Birthlayn had heard about the night in Ballater and had been waiting, since he came home, to see if he really would take that foolish pointless walk to the Downs. In his mind he went back over the conversations he'd had with people since his return, searching for small mocking inferences, and, in almost every case, hindsight revealed some maddening measure of sly sarcasm. A rage against the place of his birth welled up in him with no cure but whispered curses and cigarettes until dawn crept upon the horizon. The house was strangely silent as the old man, at some point unnoticed by Saul, had stopped snoring.

Bleary-eyed, his mouth sore from smoking, Saul decided to get a little sleep. He drank a glass of water and lay down on the daybed beside the stove. But sleep wouldn't come. He kept thinking about Mitchell and

Dorothy and the life in St. John's that was proceeding without him. And, for the first time since the war, he longed for his time on board ship, his life in the hands of his shipmates and theirs residing in him, a mutual trust and responsibility that ran deeper than anything he'd ever known, and the cold hard fact that it, too, was gone for good left him tossing and turning on the daybed, unwilling to get up and face the day feeling so terribly and awfully alone.

...

Sometimes, during those first few weeks at university, Jason Dade would often dream about the perfect girl out there somewhere, quietly preparing herself for him, as he was preparing himself for her, and he longed for the day when time and circumstance would bring them together — a meeting he deemed as inevitable as some mathematical calculation being worked out in the world's collective mind. Jennifer White turned out *not* to be that perfect girl, though she was the one who claimed his virginity.

Despite her family name, Jennifer White was dark-haired, full-breasted, plump but firm, and extremely pretty. She came from Newfoundland's west coast and Jason thought she might have some Indian blood, though he never dared to ask. She had a rather strong French accent, though she spoke no French, and he found this especially attractive. He was again too timid to inquire but he'd heard that people of French and Indian extraction, particularly on Newfoundland's west coast, had lost their language and last names — in her case probably Leblanc — to time and English culture.

It all made her seem quite mysterious and he quaked inside — once he got past merely stealing glances at her in psychology class and found the nerve to look her directly in the eye — whenever her dark eyes held his and smiled. Under her unfaltering gaze he felt himself falling backwards into some pleasurable abyss.

In a few weeks they went from friendly glances, to short conversations about their respective notes on the class, to finally concocting a plan to study together one mid-October night at the Student Centre. She clearly wasn't one of the dope-smoking crowd that he'd fallen in with, but she had no problem once they got to Jason's room with him breaking out the hash — this time it was a Turkish variety called kief — and she seemed quietly impressed with his deft handling of the drugs and paraphernalia.

He gave her the full demonstration of how to make a chillum with a soft drink can and tinfoil from a cigarette pack. Instead of using a needle or a pin, which would have been too easy, he poked holes in the foil bowl with a burned out matchstick that he'd sharpened on the brimstone of the matchbox. Then he baked a knob of acrid-smelling hash on the tip of a knife blade and waved it tantalisingly under her nose before crumbling and mixing it into precisely one-third of an Export A cigarette. He massaged it all together with a deftness and purpose that consciously mimicked his mother's bountiful fingers at home.

To light the chillum, he sucked the hot smoke manfully down into his lungs until it was fired and ready to press on to her waiting lips. They got stoned and lay on his bed. She surprised him then, responding to his first kiss by opening her mouth and offering him her tongue. She let him reach behind and clumsily undo her bra, and then — the ultimate good fortune for a shy virgin boy — she lifted her ass compliantly so he could readily pull down her jeans and raised her arms so he could ease the cotton sweater over her head and release the magnificent sway of her breasts. He scrambled out of his own clothes and kissed her again. Her surprising wetness when he entered her with his fingers, the mad insistent thrashing that ensued, seeming to demand he enter her instantly with his cock, and then her flailing and moaning once he did, all astounded him.

Afterwards, as they lay together, they closed their eyes and kissed and his tongue reached out across a moist and darkened universe before it touched sweetly down on hers.

He was looking forward to seeing Jennifer again and doing *it* again and again, so it came as a real shock when he encountered her on the steps of the Student Centre a couple of days later and found her unresponsive and gloomy. He couldn't understand her reserve toward him and concluded in his own mind, that in *her* mind, such sexual abandon as they had enjoyed had to be requited by an equal measure of guilt and shame. This baffled him. He lacked the means to dispel her gloom, so he went off and left her alone.

He never did find himself a girlfriend after that.

Jason's forefinger traces the first letter of his name in the droplets on the mirror.

J

This, for some reason, makes him think of July, the bright morning of the day he set out on the road with Chancey. He thinks of Sarah's pony in the yard, the two hundred dollars long gone, and the car accident outside Stephenville.

He raises his finger a second time and with three deft swipes forms the second letter of his name.

A

August. Hmm. Gradually losing track of time in a grim hotel room, Elvis and the switchblade, the long drive through New Brunswick, the woman in the trailer park who'd understood him so well. His hand reaches forward again.

S

September naturally follows — his arrival in North City, old Virgil and Ariadne's thread, the long wait for *something* to happen — he thinks of all that and realises, magically, that he is still writing his name.

O

October. Time spent feeling lost and disappointed ... and that horrible incident with Lenin. How could *that* be part of anybody's plan? Yet, here and now, something new and exciting *is* being revealed on the mirror. His heart beating fast, he reaches forward one last time.

N

He stares at his name etched in droplets on the glass and understands. He will not have to wait long for the next big revelation.

It will occur in November. Just as it had at university last year.

...

Ana and Saul were soon married and Saul built a new house for them on a piece of property called the Cosgrove Estate, a good ways up the road from the pond. Old Simon would have to live with them for a while yet, though Saul was hoping, with his father now in his ninetieth year, that it wouldn't be for too long. The old man was more crooked than ever, to the point that on the wedding day he chased Ana out of the house with a spruce junk in his hand. It took Saul half an hour to calm the old fucker down and let Ana come into the house. Ana, as good as gold, had taken it all in stride and there was no more trouble between them after that.

Saul was pleased he'd found a woman his own age since he wasn't interested in having an overly large family. Newfoundland was part of Canada now and he was glad of that too, knowing he'd have an easier time raising children with the help of the new baby bonus cheques, and the improvements in schools and hospitals that were already underway. Old Simon even got a few old age pension cheques out of it before he died at the age of ninety-two.

As it turned out, Saul and Ana had possibly the smallest family in the history of Birthlayn. A robust baby boy named George came first, named at Saul's insistence after the king who'd seen them through the war. The next year Ana gave birth to their second child, a "blue" baby who strengthened quickly after a difficult first few days. Saul wanted to continue his royal inclinations by naming him Charles, but Ana, for reasons she never made entirely clear, insisted on Jason. Ana prevailed again as the nineteen sixties bore down and named their only girl a biblical Sarah instead of a royal Elizabeth. After that, she became conveniently barren and Saul relaxed in the knowledge that he would be spared the rigors of raising a large family like the ones he saw ballooning around him.

Some time later Saul saw in the newspaper that Mitchell Howell, looking hale and hearty and happy, if the accompanying picture was any indication, had won himself a seat in the Newfoundland House of Assembly.

...

Luckily for Jason, multiple complaints eventually brought an official from the university Housing Office whose dire warnings were the perfect excuse to banish all intruders from his room. As a result, he started getting a little work done on his courses and, for a time, even his attendance at classes improved. Another less happy result, especially after his failed encounter with Jennifer White, was that he often found himself spending the long evenings alone. Murray Roach had given him a hit of acid, called windowpane, before leaving, so Jason decided to use one of those long evenings to "do" the acid and see what all the fuss was about.

At six o'clock he licked the tiny glass-like fragment from his fingertip and sat with his arms resting on the windowsill to gaze out at the stately facades of the residence houses. In what seemed like a short while the white globed lamps on the quad rose slowly from their black metal posts and hung suspended over silver rivers that had somehow materialised from the concrete walkways. It was as if the secret inner life of the university was being revealed to him. He expected any minute to see men in togas and women in stolas emerge and stroll between the tall white columns on the dining hall portico or gather on the steps to hear some discoursing sage. It was like the places he'd dreamed of as a boy, having fallen asleep with some illustration of antiquity from his Aunt Agnes's encyclopedia still fresh in his mind.

He pulled down the window and drew back into the room, turning to face his reflection in the full-length mirror on the door. He saw his small chair had become a throne, his army jacket a long robe, and he watched as his hair grew rapidly down over his shoulders. He stared at the mirror for a long time, utterly still, the only movement his blinking eyelids. He was just getting up the nerve to walk across the room and examine himself more closely in the mirror when he noticed that the window behind him was also being reflected in the mirror and, in *that* reflected window his reflection was being reflected again ... and so on and so on ... and he remembered when his father had taken him to Princeton for his first real haircut and the barber had held a small mirror behind so that Jason could see the back of his head reflected in the main mirror and how the mirrored images had glanced off one another like that into infinity ... and it suddenly struck him that the floor tiles that made up the distance between himself and the mirror were also being reflected and reflected and reflected into infinity and that if he did stand up and start walking on this infinity of tiles he would never get to the other side of the room no matter how long he kept walking and walking, and this thought paralysed him. Then he looked across the room and saw a bright silver sword dangling above his head, suspended from the ceiling by what looked like a long dark hair, possibly from a horse's tail, and he sat frozen with fear until the morning came, at last, and the sword gradually slipped away into thin air.

    He looked out the window and saw that the walkways had returned to concrete and the white globes had settled again on their lampposts. He decided to forget about classes for that day and crawled exhausted into bed. But sleep wouldn't come. He lay there for a long time wide awake until an old idea occurred to him. He fumbled beneath the sheets and quickly accomplished what he'd spent three long years denying himself in high school.

    That was good, he muttered, and fell off to sleep.

November

By November Jason Dade, at university, had weaned himself down to one class per week in each of his courses. He'd also formed a rough plan to prevent himself from flunking out by visiting all his profs at mid-term to offer a plausible excuse for his lack of attendance and then make an incredible comeback before final exams. But then the grant portion of his student loan came through and he suddenly found himself in possession of nearly eight hundred dollars. He cashed the grant cheque immediately and kept the full amount on him, discovering a kind of manly grace in dispensing for purchases from a thick wad of five, ten, and twenty dollar bills. He would toss the odd one to Gus, the blind man who ran the concession stand at the Student Centre, who had to rely on people's honesty when it came to knowing the denomination of bills. Jason was shocked to discover that some students were passing Gus a five and telling him it was a ten or a twenty to increase their change. He took to passing Gus a twenty and saying it was a ten.

Though his hair was still not that long Jason had finally trained it to part cleanly in the middle. It would only be a matter of time now before it began to make its way over his ears and downward on the long journey toward his shoulders. He'd given up on facial hair after several unpromising beginnings and was enjoying instead the manly, though not entirely necessary, ritual of shaving. And the khaki army jacket he'd adopted in September had been retired in favour of a more mature-looking, if slightly oversized, long black coat.

His reputation as a head had grown quickly around the residence and the Student Centre. He smoked a pack of cigarettes a day and carried a few grams of hash and a pack of rolling papers wherever he went. He always threw a nickel or a dime onto the piles of hash being smoked on the second floor of the Student Centre and he sometimes spent whole days there making conversation with anyone who cared to share a toke. As a result, he knew lots of people superficially, but remained a loner, loping through the university tunnels with his hands buried deep in his coat pockets and his inscrutable face framed, as best he could, by his hair.

The Housing Office still hadn't found him a roommate so he was enjoying what amounted to a private room. He was in his room that day in November when the first big revelation came, the one that gave him a clear insight into who he was and what was really going on in his life. He was sitting quietly with his chair tipped back and his feet resting on the desk, admiring his yellow truckin' boots. He'd spent so much of the last two months taking the underground tunnels around campus instead of walking outside that the boots, bought soon after his arrival, had kept their aura of shiny newness. The sun emerged from behind a cloud; it caressed his face and bathed the room in a warm yellow glow.

Then this happened.

He glanced over the toes of his boots at some toiletries neatly arranged on a narrow wooden shelf running above his bed along the cinderblock wall ... and the product label on his underarm deodorant pulsed with a silver light. It happened only once, a conspiratorial wink, like something you'd see on a television commercial or in a glossy magazine ad, but it didn't quite go away either and, afterwards, he couldn't help but see the label as part of some heightened new reality. Then the brand names on all the labels — toothpaste, soap, mouthwash, shaving cream — all stood out, not pulsing with silver light exactly, but swaggering somehow, proclaiming themselves to be the very best, the very latest things. And then, damned if the toes of his boots didn't, for just a second, pulse with that same silver light, and in the instant Jason felt a snapshot of himself being taken, and in the snapshot *he* was shiny and new, leaning back in his chair relaxed and happy, a smiling boy in the light-filled world of television commercials and glossy magazines.

He decided to walk over to the second floor of the Student Centre to test these strange new waters, crossing campus above ground for a change, instead of taking the tunnels. The autumn air was full of expectation, a feeling somehow enhanced by the fact that the normally bustling walkways between the academic buildings were strangely empty. He yanked open a side entrance door to the Student Centre and stepped inside. Still not a soul to be seen. The stairwell remained empty all the way up to the second floor. The dope-smoking corner was vacant, chairs in disarray, burnt out chillums lying on their sides, spilt ashes and spent matches strewn across the tables. *Where was everybody?* He walked to the railing and looked down to see that there weren't even any ping-pong or badminton players below in the gym. The building was empty, like the campus outside, yet filled with similar expectation.

A female announcer intoned softly on the student radio. A door rattled open in the gym below. A janitor with a dustpan and broom scurried along a cinderblock wall and disappeared behind a blue door as if down a rabbit hole. Jason thought of the white rabbit in *Alice In Wonderland* and immediately a bass line, familiar to him from smoke-filled nights in his residence room, crept onto the radio. *One pill makes you larger / And one pill makes you small / But the ones that mother gives you / Don't do anything at all...*

And at that precise moment he had the revelation. EVERYONE KNEW HE WAS THERE.

Everyone at the Student Centre, everyone on campus, everyone in residence, everyone at the registrar's office (he pictured operators and secretaries wearing headsets, grinning and giving each other the thumbs up — *He's got it! He's finally got it!)* likely, everyone in the whole damn university, and, probably, in one way or another, everyone in this whole section of the Avalon Peninsula, knew exactly who Jason Dade was and where he was standing at that very moment, the fact of it carried on student radio airwaves to the world.

Everyone had been waiting for him to catch on since he'd registered for university two months earlier. (They knew all about the false birth date on the application form, too, and had even chuckled a bit over it.) The moment they'd all been waiting for had come at last — the moment when Jason Dade would know he was The One.

The female radio announcer was sobbing and, with happy tears, introduced the next song.

See the man with stage fright / Standing up there with all his might / He got caught in a spotlight ...

And Jason knew the song could only be for him.

It was all a lot to take in so he decided to go back to his room and take some time alone to sort it all out. On his way back down the stairs, people came out of their hiding places with conspiratorial smiles on their faces. *Good going, Jason!"* they seemed to say. *"Good for you, boy! It's your time at last."*

He left through the same side entrance, sure that he heard a spontaneous burst of applause and cheering from inside as the door was closing behind him.

...

As November ice crystals formed nightly in the cold North City air, Jason Dade contemplated what it meant to have discovered the months of the last half of the year encrypted inside his name like a lifetime-encoded message to be unearthed at some key moment of his existence. It hadn't taken him long to notice that the first letter of his last name, D, added December to make up the sixth month. This latter realisation, however, made him wary on a couple of fronts. First of all, taking his cue from old Virgil, he was on the lookout for anagrams and was quite concerned to suddenly see that an anagram for Dade was Dead, the idea of Jason Dead being quite ominous until he remembered that the D could just as easily, even more likely, stand for Daniel, his middle name. The story of Daniel unharmed inside the lion's den, one of his favourite biblical episodes, could be embraced as a positive portent, so that, in the end, he felt safe enough.

The additional letter also suggested that his quest was likely to continue into December and this implanted another vague notion that — if he could endure yet another month of such uncertainty — the reward for all his efforts would be coincident with the arrival of a brand new year. Exactly how all that was to come about, however, remained a mystery. Still, Jason felt himself incredibly close to finding the key that would unlock the door to another great moment of understanding.

...

The road through Birthlayn takes on a silver hue in the streetlight's glare. Saul Dade feels the night air outside radiate through the windowpane. A late-summer spate of warm nights has ended, crisp autumn has come and gone, hoary winter beckons with a cold crooked finger.

Saul is brooding and smoking. He roots irritably with his forefinger into his pack of tobacco, parsing the perfect amount into a fresh rolling paper, tucks the paper expertly with his thumb and forefinger, rolls it into a neat white cylinder, and slides the faint yellow glue strip along his tongue to moisten and seal it. Then, the scrape of the match, a burst of heat and flame, his face aglow in the dark, the deep, deep inhale, and release.

He's the watcher once again, the lone sentinel in the dark house.

At first he hadn't liked the streetlight, except, of course, as a marker of progress. The children could hardly sleep it was so bright in their rooms, but they all got used to it. Now he wonders how himself and everyone else in Birthlayn had endured the darkness for so long.

Ana is asleep in their room at the opposite end of the hall on the side of the house that gives onto the meadow and the woods. The boys' room beside him is empty now. Sarah, the only child still living at home, occupies the room between.

Ana turns over in bed. Her sigh is like a distant echo on the periphery of sound. The house shifts and Saul feels something shift inside himself; the house inside him, it seems, as much as he's inside the house.

He's spent years listening at night to its hushed beating heart.

Saul has made the most, over the years, of the land that old Charlie Cosgrove had cleared and cultivated. At first resentful of the work and forever thinking on his lost opportunities in town, he'd eventually come to love the smell of soil on his hands and to take quiet satisfaction in working the land, producing good food for himself and his small family. He considered it a blessing that their survival didn't depend solely on what he could wrest from the soil, or from the sea for that matter, and eventually realised that staying in Birthlayn would not turn him into his old man. The Thunder Stone episode slipped quietly into the past and he found it was possible to be happy.

But there were trials. Periods of unemployment and financial woes had often battered at his peace, the youngsters drove him cracked sometimes, and even Ana, for all her goodness, was severely set in her ways and could leave him feeling bitter and angry after disagreements. He worked on the American base first, later in the iron ore mines of North City, and later still, on great hydroelectric projects in Bay D'Espoir and Churchill Falls. He'd gotten to a place where the youngsters were raised, all but Sarah, and where he and Ana would, in a few years, collect old age pensions that allowed them to live in a peaceful, secure, if unspectacular, retirement. That was the thing he'd been looking forward to when the business with Jason arose and threatened to suck the happiness out of everything he'd worked so long to achieve.

What in hell's flames had happened to the boy at university? What kind of a crowd had he fallen in with? He'd come home last year and hardly said two words from January to June, sitting around doing nothing, putting on weight from the hearty meals his mother insisted on putting before him, perhaps in the superstitious hope that good home cooking would cure whatever ailed him. Then in July, the boy had stopped eating altogether and began staying up all night watching the Indian head test pattern on TV.

In the end, the only thing to do was send him back into the world.

Wasn't it?

I mean, a young fellow can't stay at home forever.

...

Jason was standing outside the bunkhouse in North City staring at the stars when the second great revelation came. It flew into his mind like an arrow:

EVERYTHING HAD HAPPENED BEFORE.

From the first of July when he'd started staying up whole nights watching television, to the road trip which his father had ordained, to the mattress on the roof of the car and the accident it wrought, to Elvis and the switchblade, to the woman in the trailer park in New Brunswick who'd seemed so eerily familiar, even the recent vulgar episode with Lenin, all of it had already happened to him in exactly the same way, in exactly the same places, with exactly the same people doing exactly the same things, exactly one year ago at that exact moment in time. He realised the significance of the poem in Lenin's room — the reason he'd been sent there in the first place:

Time present and time past / Are both perhaps present in time future.

Of course they are! The present and the past coexist, occupy separate corridors in time, and, like the corridors of the bunkhouse, it is possible to travel down one to a certain point in time, and then, by a trick of the mind, come back, close off that corridor, and revisit it later on with no recollection of ever having been there in the first place and *he, Jason Dade, had done exactly that.* He was currently in the process of instinctively repeating his movements and speech from six months ago — last July 1st to December 31 — in perfectly accurate detail, every word and gesture exactly as it had happened, *and then been deliberately forgotten,* exactly one year ago. The really interesting thing was that everyone else remembered, too, and played along by repeating their own gestures and movements and words while silently observing Jason and being amazed at how he duplicated everything perfectly without the aid of memory, just on instinct alone. Jason stood transfixed as the revelation descended, then allowed himself a little smile. The challenge that would make him worthy of a second meeting with The Man was to repeat every action and word right up to the end of the current year, and the enormity of that challenge made it the longest long shot ever taken in the history of the world, a thing to redeem all past sins and failures and launch him into a new state of being.

The more immediate challenge — and this would not be easy — was to begin doing *consciously* what he had done *unconsciously* until now. He also understood that this exercise of repeating everything accurately would eventually lead him back to The Man. This time they would meet successfully and Jason's new life as The One would finally begin. On January 1st of the new year a new reality would overtake the old and Jason would be able to get out of going through all of these things twice.

O, how glorious that would be.

Yes, it was biting cold and he was underdressed, poor and alone, and a long way from home, but at last, at *long* last and against tremendous odds, the young Jason Dade was on the way to becoming the Man he was meant to be.

...

Saul Dade is standing at the window, thinking of a window from the past, a window he has lost. The lost window used to be in the pantry off the kitchen. It was the perfect height, that window, with a deep comfortable sill on which to rest his forearms as he looked out onto the meadow and the woods. He'd spent many happy hours looking through it before the seventies came along and the taste for wood paneling and new kitchen cabinetry led him to cover it up.

But he longs for that old window. It was a daydreaming window, not the night-brooding one he looks through now. It was, literally, a window for poetry and song.

You see, in those days, especially on Sundays, with the youngsters still in their church clothes lolling about the kitchen, Saul, in his white shirt and tie, with a hand-rolled cigarette between his nicotine-stained fingers, would stand at the window and fill the house with song.

Treat her kindly, Jack old pal,
And tell her I am well,
His parting words were don't forget
To give my love to Nell...

Ana would sit in the rocker and knit as the children played quietly about her feet, often building small medieval-looking towers with the splits from behind the stove.

Saul always sang with his back to them, but he would turn and face them whenever he recited *The Ballad of Lucy Grey*. The children would grow deathly quiet to hear how poor Lucy, at her father's bidding, had taken the lantern in her hand and scuffed off into a blinding winter storm. They'd be mesmerised by the time Lucy's snowy footprints disappeared at the Bridge of Wood, her ghost left behind to skip lightly across the moors, and they would ask for the ballad again and again. And Saul would usually oblige.

He can't remember now which came first — either the children stopped asking or he stopped doing it — but one way or another the little home-based tradition of his songs and recitations ended and soon after that the window on the meadow disappeared, too, as if to signify for certain that that peaceful part of his life was over for good.

...

When Jason got back to his university residence room an unpacked suitcase stood in the middle of the floor and a skinny boy with thick eyeglasses was sitting on the unused bed.

"How do you do," the boy said, extending a hand. He introduced himself with a faint lisp and a vaguely effeminate handshake: "I'm Rik without the C," he said, adding that the absent C was no big deal, and that he liked to be called just plain Rik. The Housing Office had just assigned him as Jason's roommate.

Rik went wordlessly about the business of unpacking, then sat on the bed, and in a series of minutely elegant gestures pulled a cigarette from a pack, lit it, and started smoking. An hour later they were still there, lying on their respective beds barely talking, smoking and staring aimlessly at the ceiling.

Rik said, "You wanna play cards?"

"Sure," Jason said, sensing some test or ritual being applied.

They placed a small table between the beds, their desk chairs at either end. Rik took off his shirt, revealing a bright white singlet underneath, and gave the cards a snappy shuffle. "It's called Blackjack," he said.

"The idea is to get as close to twenty-one as possible without going over. Here, we'll try a few hands for the fun of it."

They stayed up all night, then, playing for money, and by the time they heard footsteps, morning greetings, and the thrum of showers down the hall, Jason's healthy stack of bills had shrunk to a thin worrisome sheaf. Apparently deciding that the game was over, Rik wrapped an elastic band around his winnings and tossed them into a drawer. Then he pulled the curtains and got into bed.

Jason put on his long black coat and headed straight for the mall where a pretty cashier gave him a knowing look when he dropped a two-pack of white singlets on the counter. It was clear to him now that cards with Rik *was* some sort of test and the singlet was Jason's way of saying that he was ready to play.

He flashed a smile at the cashier before heading out the door.

"Good luck," she said and smiled at him.

She knew ... and she knew he knew she knew.

That night he wore a singlet and won back all his money.

...

From the moment of revelation, Jason Dade was no longer just *living* life in North City, he was *reliving* it. Every event, besides being an event in itself, also revealed exactly what had happened at that precise moment exactly one year ago. It was simultaneous exploration and discovery, mystery and revelation bound up in one moment to the next.

It was a delicate business, to be sure, but he was quickly getting the hang of it.

For example, he soon learned how, last year, he'd finally gotten out of North City.

One day at the dining hall two uniformed police officers approached and suggested Jason come for a ride in their car. He wasn't surprised when they drove him to the hospital with the washroom where he'd discovered the acronym in the mirror and led him through the large empty lobby to a door that said ADMISSIONS. Inside, he answered the nurse's questions, no doubt exactly as he'd done exactly one year ago, *and* smoking a cigarette in exactly the same way he'd done it then, *and* leaving his cigarette butt curled and broken in the ashtray in exactly the same way as last year's cigarette butt must have been. He winked at the nurse as he was leaving and he could tell she was impressed. The officers escorted him to a small ward, another nurse passed him a johnny coat, he got undressed and into bed.

It struck him that the people around him were doing a very good job of re-enacting their parts, but of course, they were merely players in small scenes; no one was undertaking anything as unbelievably complex as duplicating the entire last half of the year, as he was, but still, he couldn't resist offering them the occasional congratulatory smile. He was barely in the bed before a white-coated doctor appeared and asked him to count backwards from a hundred.

Jason hardly noticed as the needle slipped into his thigh.

Lately, Saul Dade has been paying more attention to time. He watches it creep down his cigarette and leave a crooked ash between his burnt and yellowed fingers. He watches it shroud the meadows in darkness and quiet the houses at night. He marks it in the thrusts of his saw blade and with each spray of heart wood onto the ground. He considers the exposed rings of tree stumps, marking summers and winters passed before the humans came with their greedy axes. He watches time transform the fallen trees into junks and pile them high for the splitting axe and the stove.

Standing beside the woodpile, he takes up his axe and lays a junk, not on its end, as the Americans do on television, but Irish style on its side in the V-shaped hollow of the chopping block. He raises the axe and remembers his brother Edmund's advice — *aim between the knots*. He cleaves the junk in two, quarters it, then one-hands the smaller pieces, halving and quartering them until a small pile of ivory-coloured splits lies before him. As a boy, he'd gotten so good at it that the old man growled at him for making them too thin: "It's kindling we're after," he'd say, "not toothpicks." But by then Saul had discovered the simple pleasure of seasoned wood, a well-sharpened axe, and time at the close of day. Even the old man couldn't spoil it for him after that.

"Maybe when I'm seventy," he thinks, "maybe I'll say to hell with the wood then." But Ana will resist. He knows that. She loves her wood fires and won't ever want to do without them.

"Electric heat is just not the same," she'll say, and she'll be right.

He's already accepted that the time will come when even their small house will be too much for them and they'll be better off in one of those new seniors' cottages in Princeton. But that, thank God, is not something he has to worry about tonight. He's learning not to get too far ahead of himself, learning instead to watch his thoughts run in circles without him, let them wander where they will because they always come back to where they started anyway ... to now ... to this moment ... this armload of splits brought into the house, where life will carry on and passing time will soon escape his notice once again.

He rounds the corner of the house and lingers at the edge of the incandescent glow. Through the gauze curtain he sees Ana leaning over the stove silently lifting lids from pots, moving her face away from the hot brush of steam. Past her, in the pale light of the TV, he sees Sarah turning pages, scribbling, getting her homework done. A house breathing easy for the moment, though no one seems to notice this fact but him.

Saul knows the winter will be hard; it always is. Come spring, they'll be glad to see the back of it. Yet the chill evening air has teased out some pleasant memories: crisp white snow crackling under the children's boots, gurgling water trapped under brook ice, Ana's wash stiffened on the line, or thawing in the house smelling fresh and clean, the majestic stillness of spruce trees in deep woods, youngsters pushing massive snowballs over damp snow exposing dead grass in a brown swath behind them, flocks of heart-gladdening juncos and chickadees, and best of all, the wood fires that keep his nights alive, the black winds at bay, and his family safe and warm.

But everyone isn't safe tonight and he knows it. He stands at the edge of the light, feeling alone in the stirring world. What can he do now but wrestle with the ugly fear of what time may bring? He watches his wife lift the kettle from the stove, the water pouring like liquid silver into the pot, and he's suddenly anxious to lay this gift of heat before her, the gift he cradles in his arm like a small child, and he wishes with a maddening desperation that this peaceful November moment could last, that time would stand still like this for just a little while longer.

...

After that initial blackjack game Rik lost more and more money to Jason, and Jason, for his part, spent it as fast as he could on the smokes and dope and beer and take-out food which they ultimately shared. One afternoon Rik came into the room and dropped a brown paper bag on the card table. He grinned and blinked his magnified eyes. The thick lenses rested on a nose so large that if Jason listened carefully he could hear breath coursing through the nostrils like wind through a hollow pipe.

"Aren't you gonna ask me what's in the bag?"

"What's in the bag?"

"Ten ounces of mescaline."

"... !"

"I was thinking of that naval base down there where you're from. Those American sailors make lotsa money down there. Right?"

"I dunno. I guess so."

"Well, I got the number of a sailor down there and I just spoke to him on the phone. He wants ten ounces of mescaline at $125 each. That's $1250 for the works. I went to see some guys and they said we can have these for $50 apiece. You've got $500 there, right? All we have to do is bring this load down there and drop it off. You get your money back and we split the $750.00 in profit. Not bad for a day's work." Rik went over all this with a mathematical ease, abbreviating his references to money in neat little phrases like "twelve-fifty" and "seven-fifty" and "one-twenty-five", puffing the while on the cigarette he held casually between his fingers.

"When?" Jason asked.

"We can head down there tomorrow if you like. I was thinking we could stay with your folks overnight and come back the next day. I've got the drop all set up. So what do you say? You in or what?"

"Sure," said Jason.

Jason opened the bag to see the mescaline organized into ten tightly-knotted clear plastic bags. He was surprised by its flaky texture until Rik explained that it had been cut with Carnation instant milk powder. To share the risk evenly they would carry five bags each. The bags, roughly the size of baseballs, would fit easily enough inside the deep pockets of their winter coats. Jason handed over the five hundred and Rik went off to conclude that part of the deal.

The next day at noon they took up their place in a long line of hitchhikers already gathered on Kenmount Road. Luckily, a steady stream of cars was exiting the city and it wasn't long before their turn came up and a big green station wagon pulled to the curb. The driver, short-haired, short-sleeved, and clean-shaven, turned out to be a born-again Christian who took great delight in telling the story of his personal salvation while manoeuvring his powerful car through traffic and basically passing everything in sight. Jason sat up front with the driver while Rik pretended to doze off in the back. The time passed quickly enough and Mr. Christian barely had time to end the tale of his teary-eyed acceptance of Jesus before he pulled over at the Princeton crossroads and let them out.

"Thank Jesus that's over," Rik quipped, as the station wagon pulled away.

They looked down the access road, quickly swallowed up in the ragged forest that surrounded them, and for the next two hours put out hopeful thumbs with no luck. It was getting dark and Rik was just proposing to call it quits and try heading back to town when a car finally pulled over.

"Going to make a killing on the slot machines, are ya?" the driver joked, when he learned they were going to the naval base.

"Not likely," Jason tersely replied.

He was stuck in the front seat again but determined this time not to encourage conversation. This proved a bad decision, since the driver, disappointed by the lack of enthusiasm for banter, took an early turn into Princeton and left them by the side of the road an hour's walk from the security gate.

"I should've buttered him up," Jason lamented. "I bet he would've taken us right there."

"Fuck 'im!" said Rik.

It was dark now and to make matters worse the wind ramping off the ocean bore the first flakes of a thick watery snowfall. Jason was glad for his winter coat and huddled deep inside it as they scrunched their way along the gravel shoulder toward the gate. Neither of them had thought to bring a hat or gloves. When the sentry gate finally appeared up ahead, they ducked into the woods to rearrange their bags of mescaline, studying each other to make sure it looked like they had nothing more than a pair of gloves or a wool hat stuffed into their pockets. It occurred to Jason that the sentry might wonder why, on a night like this, they weren't wearing the supposed hats and gloves, but he said to hell with it. He'd often heard how slack the base security could be.

"Just tell the guard you're going to the Windjammer," he told Rik. "You'll have to fill out a form and, fuck, now that I think of it you have to leave a piece of ID."

"ID?"

"Proof of age," said Jason.

"How old do you have to be to get in there?"

"Drinking age."

"Twenty-one?"

"Yes, twenty-one. Why? How old are you anyway?"

"Nineteen," Rik replied.

"But you have a fake ID, right?"

"No. Do you?" Rik hunched for shelter under the alders, sniffing, and blinking his enormous wet eyes. The snow already pasted to his hair made him look like a decrepit little red-faced old man. "'Cause if you don't, we're screwed," he added.

"What day is this?" asked Jason.
"It's Thursday. Why?"
"No, the date. The day of the month."
"The thirtieth."

Jason pulled out his wallet. It was his birthday. It amazed him that he had somehow overlooked it, but he was delighted to have this chance to make use of his infallible false ID. His stiff frozen hand was holding solid proof that he'd just turned twenty-one instead of seventeen. He took this as further confirmation that he was to take charge of the entire enterprise.

"Give me your dope," he said. It took a few minutes to arrange the extra load so as not to arouse suspicion. Then he asked Rik for the particulars of the drop-off.

"He'll be at slot machine number three," Rik assured him. "Just ask, 'Are you Number Three?' and if he answers 'Who else would I be?' then he's our man. Got it?"

"Wait for me under that old railway trellis," Jason said. "I'll be back with the money in a couple of hours."

...

Jason awoke from his sedation with his brother George standing on one side of the hospital bed and a pleasant-looking man in a beige trench coat standing on the other.

"Jason," George said, "this here is Constable Sullivan of the RCMP."

"Oh, good," said Jason. "He's here to take me back to St. John's."

George and Constable Sullivan exchanged glances.

That little son of a gun.

Jason smiled drowsily at his own cleverness and then fell right back to sleep.

George felt miserable leaving the hospital, though he hadn't been all that surprised when the cops showed up at his door. It was only a matter of time before Jason and his antics had come to their attention. Someone at the bunkhouse, or maybe the dining hall, where he also spent inordinate amounts of time, had complained. And he knew it was for the best to have Jason put into some kind of protective custody, but he'd still found it hard to sign those goddamn papers. There was nothing else for it, he consoled himself. The time had come to act.

Now he wondered how he was going to tell the old man.

...

Sarah is in bed with the light on reading about Don Quixote. She has occasionally come across the strange word "quixotic" in her reading and tonight, in her Aunt Agnes's encyclopedia she's discovered that it refers to a man named Don Quixote ... in her mind she pronounces it *quix-oat*. She's reading the article in volume D-E and knows now about the man who went crazy reading books and she knows that huge hopeless gestures — such as buying your baby sister a horse against your father's wishes when you're only a boy yourself — are named after that man. There's a picture of the man on his horse; both horse and man look weary and frightened.

A man with a trailer hitch came today and took Sarah's pony away. She's sad but she's always known somehow that the pony couldn't stay. It's not practical, they don't have a proper stable, and it's not fair for her parents to have to look after it. She understands that it wasn't right for Jason to bring a horse into the family without asking permission, and she's known all along that the pony could stay only as long as her father allowed it. She and her father have never talked about it. But a man came today just the same and now the horse is gone. It's just the way things are.

Sarah never had to be told how to ride a pony. She was naturally capable of approaching that skittish beast in an open meadow, clutching its mane in her fists and leaping onto its bare back. She was the only one in Birthlayn who could do it. But a pony costs money to keep and feed and, with winter coming on, it needs a proper place to get in out of the weather.

Sarah hopes the new owner will be kind.

She's determined to read the whole encyclopedia over time, from A to Z just like Jason did. She wonders where is he tonight. She knows he's up north somewhere; he didn't even call home on his birthday. He should be happy, celebrating somewhere; even if birthdays were never allowed to be a big deal in their house, at least there was always a card with some American money in it from Aunt Agnes. There was one for him there now on the table in the hall.

The house is quiet at night, especially now that Jason and George are both gone. It's as if she can hear it breathe. She likes the peace and quiet, though it's lonely sometimes. She worries about Jason and wonders if it was a good idea for him to go to North City. She remembers the night of his birthday one year ago today, the night he'd tried to come home. She remembers a stirring in the yard, her father hopping out of bed to stride down the hall and snap on the kitchen light.

Soaking wet and freezing, Jason approached slot machine number three in the Windjammer Lounge. It was being played by a tall black man, lean and lanky with large relaxed hands. He wasn't in uniform, though Jason could easily imagine him in a white sailor's cap and baggy blue trousers, dutifully carrying out his chores about the base. It was around ten o'clock and the barroom was filled with casual chatter and the low shuffle of feet. Dull-eyed patrons mindlessly pulled the levers of the one-armed bandits along the wall, exercising a practiced, hopeful calm as the fruit-filled reels spun time and again to their seemingly inevitable disappointment. Occasionally, a metallic slush sent a small payout into the change drawer.

The contact barely glanced up when Jason approached.

"Are you Number Three?"

"Who else would I be?" the fellow replied, and suddenly the game was on.

After taking time to methodically drop the last of his quarters into the slot machine, Number Three stood up and, with a look that dramatically emphasised the whites of his eyes, indicated an exit door to the rear. Jason followed him outside onto a large wooden deck that was, thankfully, in the lee of the building. Jason's ears had gone completely numb on his walk from the gate and a few minutes thawing in the lounge had set them on fire. He was looking forward to emptying his heavy-laden pockets and getting enough cash in return to hire a taxi all the way to Princeton, pick up Rik along the way, and spend the night in a warm and comfortable hotel.

He never had any intention of staying at his parents' house.

Everything seemed to be going according to plan as Number Three led Jason down a wide staircase off the balcony and across a strip of beach into the lee of yet another building. Snowflakes blew at a sharp angle across the pale glare of a lone streetlight. Jason assumed the time had come, and took a couple of the bags out of his pockets. Holding one in each hand, he was struck by the realisation that Number Three clearly didn't have room for all ten bags in the small bomber jacket he was wearing. The plan, he assumed, was to stash them somewhere nearby for pick-up later.

Then *this* happened.

Number Three looked nervously around, shrugged his bomber jacket up off his hip and hiked out his wallet. He removed an American twenty dollar bill and held it toward Jason. It flapped gingerly in the wind. Jason thought of the American money his Aunt Agnes had sent him over the years tucked inside birthday cards. Maybe there was one at the house for him now.

"Do you have change for a twenty?" the man said.

At this strange question, a rivulet of cold snot escaped Jason's nose and slid helplessly down his lip.

Half an hour later, back at the rendezvous point, he broke the bad news to Rik.

"Twelve dollars and fifty cents! He offered you *twelve dollars and fifty cents* for ten ounces of mescaline?"

"You were the one who said *twelve-fifty*, Rik! You always talk about money in abbreviations. *One twenty-five. Twelve-fifty.* He obviously thought you meant ten *hits* of mescaline, not ten whole bags!"

Rik guffawed. "Must be giant fuckin' pills then!" he said, gesturing weirdly with his hands to mime swallowing the oversized capsules. "*Must be Alice-in-Fucking- Wonderland-sized pills.*"

"You should have been clearer on the phone!"

"So, it's *my* fault." Rik's face was as red as a beet, his nose in full flood.

"Yes! Now, shut up and follow me. I'm going to have to get us out of this mess."

They set off on foot toward Princeton. Jason was undaunted; in fact, he was feeling more like a movie star than ever, on the run with his hapless sidekick, trudging this desolate road in a snowstorm with enough chemicals in their possession to land them both in serious trouble; this was juicy danger, and only a man's wits and survival instincts would get them out of it. Clearly, this was a test to see if he could be that man.

He was uneasy, though, because it looked like he had no choice now but to go home. It was either that or sleep in the woods. The main thing was to get back to St. John's as quickly as possible, return the drugs, and hope that Rik's dealers won't be too pissed off. Rik, shivering uncontrollably, looked on the verge of collapse. "We've got to keep moving," Jason said, grabbing him dramatically by the arm and pulling him into the wind. There was nothing for it now but to walk the seven long miles to Birthlayn and call on his father's good sense and generosity to let them spend the night in Jason's room.

After the first unbearable hour they made it to Princeton beach. The old courthouse loomed through the drift like a ghostly apparition. The wind mercifully shifted to their backs as they stumbled up the beach road. At length they turned onto the slope of the Blockhouse Hill and crept along for another mile or two in the meagre shelter of the tree-lined ridge.

Jason slipped into a reverie of hot suppers cooked for him long ago. He remembered walking home from basketball practice in winter playing a guessing game with himself as to which of his mother's hot, filling, tasty dishes would be warming for him in the oven; how savoury and delicious they were when he finally arrived, his mother having laid it all out for him on the table like a feast, and he would eat and eat to his heart's delight and finish with a cup of strong sweet tea and perhaps a slice of his favourite pie, or he might munch happily on two or three of his mother's date squares piled high on a plate before him, or ....

"How much further?"

Rik.

"I'll fucking die if I have to stay out in this much longer."

Jason was all business now. "Hey!" he shouted, "it's your fault we're in this fucking mess. I should leave you to freeze in a ditch."

He would never do that, of course, but the exhilaration of venting his anger actually warmed him.

Finally, they came to the height of the land and started trudging towards the open sea and down into

Birthlayn, once again facing the full brunt of the storm. Rik staggered a couple of times and Jason, dreading the thought of actually having to carry him, called encouragement; somehow the reluctant apprentice kept plodding along in silence.

The house, at last, came into view. Everything was dark when Jason quietly opened the gate, but the kitchen light snapped on the second they stepped in the yard.

...

Constable Sullivan hardly said a word to Jason on the flight out of North City. He watched nervously as his charge bounced about the cabin of the plane chatting with passengers. Jason wanted to let them know that, as The One in the midst of this enormous challenge, he wasn't going to let them down. After all, they'd all taken the trouble to get on the same flight as a year ago. Same people. Same seats. Same food. Same departure time. Same turbulence (amazing). Same arrival.

A car was waiting at St. John's airport. Jason and the constable strode outside into a black windy night and climbed aboard. Jason sat up front with the driver, the constable silent in the back. It occurred to Jason that the constable might actually be taking him to a big swanky hotel to meet The Man, but there was no telling for sure, so he stayed mum on the point and bided his time. What happened last year at this moment and the next and the next was being revealed in any case. The taxi eventually manoeuvred up a long driveway to a gloomy red-bricked building with a worn Victorian façade.

Could The Man be staying here?

The constable got out and opened the car door. Jason stepped agreeably out, sucking in the damp night air. A loose debris of chip bags and ice-cream wrappers blew about his feet as they walked up the broad concrete steps and through a double set of glass doors which banged heavily shut behind him. A large rat scurried up the steps and looked dolefully through the glass before retreating into the windblown night.

There followed a rush of pale green corridors awash in fluorescent light. Jason noticed that the constable had suddenly disappeared and that he was flanked instead by two stocky men in pale green short-sleeved smocks. They stood close and half guided, half steered him through a network of polished hallways. Finally, they stood in front of a door with a small wire-meshed window through which Jason observed the grim approach of a female nurse holding a large silver key. The snap and slide of the deadbolt made him realise what was going on.

"Fuck this," he announced, "I'm leaving."

But one of the attendants put him in a chokehold, then steered him through the door and down the corridor at a fast clip. Jason, in a helpless fury, screamed dire threats: *I will fuckin' kill you! I will tear this fucking place to the ground!*

Another door flew open and in he went, another deadbolt snapped and he turned to see an attendant's face grinning at him through another wire-meshed window. He punched the glass viciously with his fist, gratified to see the face recoil in fright.

Jason opened the kitchen door to see his father standing beside the wood stove in boxer shorts and a yellowed singlet, a sleepy look about him, a lock of iron grey hair thrust up on his crown like a kingfisher's plume. The arms folded across his chest and the resolution in his father's look told Jason immediately that he and his accomplice were being denied access to the inner reaches of the house.

"Hello, Father."

Jason glanced down to see water drip madly out of his coat and slide unerringly toward the corner where, as a child, their marbles had always rolled whenever they played with them on the impossibly uneven floor.

After a brief stony silence Saul asked, "Who's this?"

Rik removed his glasses and stepped forward into the kitchen squinting and sniffing like a laboratory rat. "The name is Rik, without the C," he said, and to Jason's amazement actually extended a hand.

"Get out," Saul said. "The pair of you."

They eventually took refuge in a stable. It was dry at least, with an encouraging animal warmth. They entered and a milk cow struggled to her feet with a snort of protest. Three more gradually appeared out of the darkness, the air a pungent mix of manure, dry hay and milky breath. Jason knew the stable; he'd often stowed hay there as a boy. He knew the hay bulk, into which he'd often made boyhood somersaults, lay behind the door to his right; the loft where they would sleep was directly over their heads.

He groped for the cord that activated the latch,

gave it a tug and felt the door to the bulk fall open against his foot.

"This way," he whispered.

Rik, who'd lapsed into a grim silence since leaving the house, shuffled obediently in behind. Jason made out the high-placed shutters and remembered pitchforks of hay bursting through them to fall into waiting arms. He was surprised to see how much the hay in the bulk was already depleted. He hadn't realised how quickly it disappeared once the cows were done with grazing and relied instead on the hay put daily in their mangers.

Jason reached out and touched the ladder he'd scrambled up so often to the loft. As he climbed he imagined the soft, sweet smelling hay where he and Rik would finally get some sleep. He was disappointed to find it cold, soured, and matted into dense layers. Instead of pulling the loose cozy stuff around him, as he'd so often done in play, he could only crawl miserably between the matted layers and direct his shivering companion to do the same.

December

As far as the youngsters were concerned, December was a marvellous time in Birthlayn. The early evening darkness, which tended to distress the adults, made the place seem even more mysterious and strange. Whether it was sliding, building forts for snowball wars, or skating and hockey on the pond, no one ever wanted to stop winter play until it was just too dark to continue. Then, golden light from kitchen windows would guide them through the black night home. Often, after skating all day, the youngsters' feet were so cold and tired they couldn't bring themselves to unlace their skates and instead walked up the road with their skates on, sending tiny yellow sparks flying off the silver blades into the dark. Sometimes, when little Jasie was trudging home alone he found guidance and comfort in those sparks and the muffled voices ahead of him on the road, though he would never wear his own skates on the road, since every pair he'd ever owned had entered his life from under a Christmas tree. Skates always seemed like something to be kept shiny and new, especially to a boy growing so fast that he needed a fresh pair ever other year. Thankfully, George was usually there to unlace and pull off the skates for him whenever his own hands were too stiff and frozen for the job.

  He and George and Sarah would tramp through the yard and into the small crowded porch, their pants legs and mittens clogged with snow, and stand there while Ana gave them a through brushing with the broom. Little Jasie loved how the broom strokes magically made the snow disappear, broken straws flying off and littering the porch floor. Then the kitchen door was thrown open and they stepped into the warmth. Sarah and Georgie hung their skates up in the porch, but Jasie insisted on bringing his inside and, once the ice had melted from the blades, wiping them clean and dry and hanging them on the hook his father had put up beside the coat rack, especially for him.

...

It was past midnight when Jason finally grew tired of punching the meshed glass and kicking the door, screaming curses at people he could no longer see, so at last he lay down on the floor. At that exact moment, the door popped open and a grey wool blanket and a pillow were tossed inside. He couldn't bring himself to give in to sleep before one last bout of screaming and so lay there, a blue gym mat his bed, as his rage-filled cries stirred muffled replies from deep within the building's walls. The corridor outside suddenly went dark and, at last, exhausted by the howling and thrashing, he fell asleep.

When he awoke new faces appeared in the window, an assortment of curious onlookers who leaned in for a look at him before meandering on their chatty way. Most were blandly satisfying their curiosity, but a calloused few displayed an inane delight at the sight of this crouched and scowling boy. His fists were too sore to punch the glass anymore, so Jason satisfied himself by pacing the cell and occasionally giving them all the finger. It seemed a morning and afternoon passed before he tired again. He crawled out of view of the window as best he could and, with barely enough presence of mind to pull the blanket around him, fell off again to sleep.

When next he woke up a pair of light green cotton pyjamas lay on the floor. Both the tail of the shirt and the seat of the pyjama bottoms bore the inked inscription Property of Waterford Hospital, displayed in a blue circular design like you'd see on slab of pork.

So.

It was true.

He was in The Mental.

Again the question: *How could this be part of anybody's plan?*

But even as this thought occurred, other ideas readily provided a reason and rationale for his being in this most unlikely of places.

Certainly, from a biblical point of view, it was not inappropriate for The One to be in such humble, even demeaning, surroundings. Christ was born in a stable after all.

The new sleepwear smelled fresh and clean. As he slipped it on he saw that the soles of his feet were black and there was dirt between his toes. He suddenly realised it had been a while since he'd taken a shower.

And he was hungry.

...

Saul's face is at the windowpane again, the one in the hall, watching December wind rip across the land, bearing large wet snowflakes from off the sea. He looks deep into the maelstrom and contemplates these particular snowflakes chosen from all the other countless snowflakes whirling out there to sail across *his* eye in this moment, to ride in off the ocean and die with barely audible thumps on the windowpane inches from *his* face, their wild hysterical arcs reminding him of the kamikaze pilots that had haunted his dreams back when he was a sleeping sailor on a ship. Everything so random, so arbitrary, so ridden with chance.

Saul Dade rarely drinks alone. Usually, he's at a bar or maybe, occasionally, at someone else's house. But tonight he said fuck it and on the way home from Princeton he stopped into the liquor store on the beach and bought a bottle. It's only just past midnight and the bottle is three-parts gone. And so is he. He's never been able to pace himself with drink.

But the desired effect has been achieved. He finds he's ready now to do the crazy thing that he's been wanting to do all week.

...

Morning came to the stable. Rik slept feverishly as Jason, through the floorboards, watched his cousin Jimmy feed the cows. Jimmy came later to milk them as well, both boys watching silently from above. Then darkness came again and the stowaways slipped out the stable door and down the lane and walked all the way back to Princeton.

Jason spotted a police car in Princeton and became very worried about all the drugs they were carrying. He was more anxious than ever to get off the road and make a fast return to the city.

Luckily, at the Esso station he came upon the perfect means of escape.

"There's no room in the cab," the tow-truck driver explained, "but you can crawl in under there if you like." A stiff tarpaulin curled around the base of his tow hook. He probably meant it as a joke — the wind was already brutally cold and a powdery snowfall was thickening the night sky — but Jason saw it as an ideal way to get back to town undetected. They crawled under the tarpaulin in the bitter cold and, for the first time in the whole expedition, clung to one another for warmth.

When they staggered wearily into the residence three hours later, Rik, sicker than ever, insisted on going straightaway to return the dope and ask for the money back. He returned in high dudgeon once the dealers had refused.

"Fuck them," he said, his face ashen with rage and fever. "*Fuck* them! I'll show those cocksuckers what I think of their shitty fuckin' drugs."

With that he un-knotted a bag and started pouring it into his mouth. He was chewing and swallowing the stuff and soon his lips and chin were covered in it. He must have done forty or fifty hits right there.

"The least you can do is help me out," he said, and shoved a bag at Jason.

Jason felt the grit and grind of that powder on his teeth for weeks.

Afterwards, they stayed in the room for days without eating. They didn't talk or play music, just sat there, slumped against the wall or lying on their beds, thinking. Not even thinking, really. Just being. Eventually, Jason found himself turning a matchstick in the fingers of his right hand over and over for hours on end ... *tick-tock, tick-tock, like the seconds on a clock* ... it turned and he watched, detached, as if time itself propelled the match forward and not him at all ... time itself, right there in his hand ... turning ... turning ... turning.

In the end, Rik grew so pale and weak that Jason became afraid and took him to the Student Clinic. It turned out he had pneumonia. At least, that's what the nicely-penned note on the desk said that evening when Jason came back to the empty room.

Apparently, Rik's parents had come and taken their son back home.

...

After a couple of good sleeps on his gym mat, Jason felt better equipped to take stock of his situation. There was, he decided, no real need for alarm — he was where he was and that's all there was to it — though it *was* time to get out of that room. After all, the only way to find out what had happened this time last year was to simply let it happen again. As a goodwill gesture he carefully folded his discarded clothes, laid them in the centre of the room, sat back and waited.

Eventually, the door swung open and one of the burly attendants filled the doorway.

"It's dinnertime," he said. He had a cheerful round face and dark slicked-back hair. The smell of his after-shave brought Jason back to the night of his "arrival," but he decided to rise above those past indignities and carry on.

"Take me to your leader," he said, and marched through the door.

So far so good.

The wide corridor outside roiled like a city street. Patients walked briskly down one side of it and up the other in a tidy circular flow, hopping on and off at the intersecting corridor as if it was a streetcar stop. The inmates — proper word, Jason decided, since no one could pass beyond that locked door without permission — were dressed in pyjamas like himself, though some seemed to have added personal touches, such as their own bathrobe and slippers. A few had on ill-fitting pants and shirts with the stamp of the institution prominently displayed. One tall skinny fellow wore shorts and cowboy boots, eerily exposing the veins of his virtually translucent legs. Another chap, bearded and weary-looking, wore an Edwardian-style smoking jacket. Others, mostly in terrycloth bathrobes, walked arm in arm as gaily as if they were at a garden party or parading at a high school prom. A blue haze of cigarette smoke hung over these proceedings.

Jason was impressed by how perfectly everyone was ignoring him. He might as well have been invisible. In a way, he enjoyed not being the centre of attention for a change. That said, there wasn't much else to like about the place. A vaguely unpleasant odour exuded from everything, including the inmates themselves, and before long Jason found himself looking toward his locked cell door with a peculiar sense of longing.

The locked door to the outside corridor swung open suddenly and a tall man, confused, unshaven and stark naked was trotted forcibly down the corridor by two hefty attendants. Everyone laughed and pointed at the exposed genitals before the poor fellow was tossed unceremoniously into the cell that Jason had just vacated. To show just what he thought of that, Jason walked into the crowded lunch room, loaded up his tray with food and then kicked the whole thing into the air with a loud disruptive clatter.

No one even bothered to look up.

...

Saul tears open the hallway door with a loud resisting creak. The house responds with a gasp, this door so rarely opened at all, and never in winter. Saul in the middle of the storm, stumbling through blinding snow and howling wind, even light from the houses obscured, somehow finds his way down the hill, and then to the Downs Road where he crosses the narrow wooden bridge between the ponds and enters the Groves.

He's surprised by the clearing at the top of the rocky lane, then remembers that youngsters had started playing ball in the Groves some years ago. It's all changed since his day and this makes him feels hopeless for a moment until he finds an old crumbling grey fence to show him a way into the woods. His arms flail against the snow-filled branches as he forges his path, trying not to lose sight of the fence. It fails him eventually but he blunders on, unguided, finding his way through the fury and freezing cold, until the hard resisting spectre of the lesser thunder stone strikes abruptly against his hands. He takes strange comfort from its abrasive touch, like the playful feel of a father's unshaven face against a young boy's cheek. Seeking shelter in the lee of the stone, he trips and falls in the narrow trench he'd dug himself all those years ago. Defeated, he lays miserably on the ground and starts to cry.

"You said there'd be good things ... you said ... everything ... you said ... I'd find *everything* I needed ... *good things* ... not this ... not *this*...".

He gets to his feet and slams his fists into the unforgiving stone, recoils in pain, then slumps soaked and shivering against it.

He hears a voice on the wind ... *father ... father...* distant, then snatched away. He shivers uncontrollably, tired, drunk, and freezing. He knows he must get himself home. The voice carries again on the wind ... *father... father...*

And suddenly George is at his side. He'd arrived late from North City and found Ana at home, frightened and worried. He braved the storm to go in search, feeling lost and hopeless himself until he'd come to the bridge of wood between the ponds.

That's where he'd spotted his father's footprints in the snow.

...

Jason knew he could never go home like Rik. And he knew his parents would never come for him. They understood that he had to be left alone, that he had important work to do. Soon there would be an important meeting with a very important Man and in that meeting one of the most important transactions in the history of the world would take place. The time had come for the Old World of Europe and the New World of North America to finally be united. Jason Dade had a vital role to play in bringing about that cosmic union.

He was to be The One, the youthful representative of the New World, and The Man would be his elder counterpart from the Old World. Together, they would unite the old and new. Newfoundland was the perfect place for their meeting — after all, her very geography and geology resulted from the separation of the two continents — and Jason was the perfect one, *The One* in fact, to embody all that was new in the New World.

He was the very latest thing.

No one told him these things. They'd come to him slowly, as revelations, until, one day, he just *knew* the time had come.

And that's why he went to the bar on that fateful night.

...

Jason was learning the routines of the hospital: up and out at 8:00 a.m., no sleeping in allowed; the horrible breakfast choices: lukewarm porridge and cold dry toast, sawdust cereal drowned in watery milk, a large silver pot filled with the unappetizing prospect of rapidly cooling hard-boiled eggs; then, at ten, the medication, distributed mid-morning and mid-afternoon from a little silver pushcart where the inmates lined up and dumbly waited to swallow down their personal cluster of pills. Of course, *he* wasn't getting any medication — for obvious reasons. This was followed by lunch, and then, after a long monotonous afternoon, supper comprised of tepid soup and other things lukewarm — turnip, carrot, mashed potato, plus deplorable renderings of meat, chicken and fish — all compartmentalised on a flimsy plastic tray.

He marvelled at the way the others wolfed it down. He spent a lot of time in the TV room, sometimes dozing off in one of the big chairs. He rarely spoke and no one said much to him. He had a comfortable bed on a ward now, with clean sheets and a decent pillow. Every couple of days an attendant showed up with a pair of folded white towels and led him to a shower room. A pair of cotton beige pants and a pale blue shirt had been waiting for him after one shower, along with a pair of red Converse sneakers like the ones he'd worn playing basketball in high school. It crossed his mind that they might be the very same pair ... that they had been saving them for him. If so, he was unimpressed.

And so ... he waited, keeping a weather eye on how the time was passing.

During his second or possibly his third week there, a fiftyish woman in plainclothes, presumably a nurse, though she struck him as more of a nun, approached him in the television room and quietly said that a certain Dr. Alderdice was making his rounds that day and would very much like to have a talk with Jason. Jason decided this might be helpful and agreed to an appointment that afternoon. Dr. Alderdice turned out to be a small wiry Scotsman with straw-coloured hair who scrunched in his chair and grimaced as he scrutinized Jason and asked him silly questions: Did Jason know where he was? What year were they in? (!) Who was Prime Minister of Canada? How did he feel about his situation in general? Jason answered all the questions carefully and, apparently, exactly as he'd done one year ago and Dr. Alderdice seemed satisfied.

The next day the nun approached and said that Dr. Alderdice had prescribed some pills. Jason thought this a bit odd — why would *he* need pills? — but he decided to play along and the next time the silver pushcart came around he stood in line and washed down the contents of the little crushable paper cup like everybody else. But the pills made him sleepy and caused him to nod off during the day, and he often had the unpleasant sensation of small electric shocks firing in his brain, and he told the nun lady and Dr. Alderdice about this and the next day Jason's name wasn't called when the silver pushcart came around. And the little electric shocks stopped and he started feeling better all round.

One day Jason was in the lunchroom sipping a glass of milk when he looked up and saw his father standing in the doorway. He quickly decided his best course was to play dumb and ignore him. Saul made no attempt to speak to him either, which seemed to confirm the wisdom of Jason's choice. Best for all concerned to say nothing. Yet. Best to wait until everything is completed. Then the joyous celebrations could ensue.

His father quietly conferred with the nun-nurse, then left.

...

Imagine you are walking through your own brain. Picture it as a huge mansion, an elaborate maze of corridors, rooms, stairways and doors. You walk and walk and walk until at last you arrive at the top of a narrow stairwell that leads to a door. You descend that stair and open that last door into a dark, musty, cramped and claustrophobic room. There are no more rooms in the house, no more doors to be opened, no more corridors to walk down. You are at the very centre of your own being. It's dark, so you strike a match and look around. You see stacks of boxes and papers and old trunks, and you realise they contain the darkest, most dearly held secrets of the generations of people who have lived in this house and to which you are now the heir. All this, whether you want it or not, belongs to you. It is part of you and it will someday be part of your own legacy. It is the truth.

Knowledge is power and knowledge of another person's truth is powerful indeed. Therefore, to hand this personal truth of yours to another, to voluntarily give them that power over you, would be the action of a fool. And this is the terrifying thing about the moment when The Man and The One meet, for in that moment they must be such fools. Each must open the door to his secret inner self and trust the other not to look inside.

It can take a long time for The One and The Man to locate each other in the world, but when the meeting finally does occur, the place should be neutral, belonging to neither The Man nor The One, and with other people in attendance. This is why a barroom is an ideal choice. In that setting, Man and One can recognize or ignore each other to the degree they deem it proper. They can overhear each other talk and look each other over and, all the while, if they so wish, maintain the illusion that none of it is really happening.

The barroom must be carefully selected. Good barrooms are places of ritual. They are a proving ground for humour, wit, and intelligence; yes, even chivalry and honour can be put to the test within the confines of a public house. A proper Man must know how to conduct himself in a bar. He must never imbibe to the point of humiliating intoxication. He must never talk like a fool, nor spend like one. A proper Man chooses a bar befitting his station. The persons in the bar must be intelligent and well-dressed, the conversation tasteful, the service impeccable, the lighting subtle, the liquor expensive and good. And if it is not such a place, then it must be imbued with these qualities by the people who inhabit it, to the best of their ability. A bar is meant to be more than a conduit to debauchery. In a good bar, a Man can display his finer qualities: even-handedness, verbal elegance, self-control, etiquette, wit, chivalry and generosity. In a good bar, it is not only possible, but essential, to be a gentleman.

However, the meeting in the bar is merely the prelude to the main event. It is the amazing thing that happens after the meeting, after the bar closes and The Man and The One have gone to their respective abodes, that determines if the meeting was really a success or no.

...

"Virgil!"

Jason's old cohort from North City was standing there in the corridor wearing a blue terrycloth bathrobe and a comfortable looking pair of wool-lined suede slippers.

"I was wondering when I'd run into you," Virgil said. "C'mon, let's go somewhere and talk."

And so they did, in the big lounge opposite the television room where the ward's occasional visitors were entertained.

"You look at home," Jason said lightly as they sat down. Virgil offered him a ready-made cigarette, which was nice because Jason had been relying on tobacco and rolling papers supplied by the hospital for the last few weeks.

"I come prepared," Virgil said. "I'm an old hand at this racket."

"You did say that you'd been where I was going," said Jason.

"That's right," said Virgil. "I've been here many times, usually for a night or two until they figure out what to do with me."

"What's the matter?"

"You don't know?"

"No."

"Well, I need some help to stop drinking for a while, that's all."

"Oh, I see."

Virgil laughed. "You see, do you? Well, how about you then? Have you figured it all out yet or what?"

"The way I see it everything becomes clear on New Year's Day."

"Do you think so?"

"Yes, I have a feeling it'll be right around then."

It occurred to Jason that this conversation with Virgil had taken place one year ago as well but he found himself only vaguely interested in the idea — *perhaps part of the whole process of coming into real time?* The end of the year was in sight; the long shot was almost done. All he had to do was wait it out.

"You look good," Virgil said. "You may not have to wait that long even."

"How long?"

"You know, until New Year's. Something might happen before then."

"I never thought of that," said Jason, "but it would be nice. I'd just like it to be over and done with now."

"It won't be long," said Virgil. "You'll get there."

"I figured out about my name and the last half of the year, you know."

Virgil paused for a second, then laughed. "J-A-S-O-N ..."

"And D for Daniel," said Jason, "... and for December, of course."

"You're a bright fellow, Jason. That's how I know you'll get all this sorted out in the end. After all, it's only a matter of time."

And they laughed conspiratorially at that little joke.

"Daniel in the lion's den," said Virgil.

"That's me," said Jason.

"Yes, you're in the lion's den now, my son, but I predict you will emerge unscathed."

...

Christmas in the Mental was quiet and unspectacular. There were no presents, though Jason did receive a card from his mother. He hoped she knew that everything was okay, that he had it all under control. On Christmas Day Jason watched the snow pile in delicate flakes on the red-bricked windowsills outside and gather ever so gently on the twigs and branches of the darkened trees. He spent the evening just sitting in the lounge with the television off as inmates shuffled past the doorway in the subdued light of the corridor.

Christmas music played distantly on the PA and a few thin red garlands hung from the walls. It was lonely but he consoled himself that he could probably count the days until the new meeting with The Man would be done, this *re*-living everything would end and *real* life would start all over again.

...

Jason walked into the St. John's bar that December night and recognized The Man immediately. He could tell it was Him by the physically imposing presence, the tasteful clothes, the rich timbre of his voice as he talked and laughed with his coterie. Jason marched up to present himself but suddenly found, to his great surprise, that he couldn't think of anything to say. He just stood there in front of The Man, speechless. All along he'd pictured the meeting as involving some really clever verbal exchanges, and he was confounded to find himself incapable of coming up with a single word. The longer he stood there the worse it got. The Man seemed mildly put off and turned his back. Jason, hoping for the best, turned on his heels and left the bar. Shortly after, he took up with a group of casual acquaintances going to a party at a nearby apartment. It was there, about an hour later, that Jason felt something shifting inside his head, a kind of electrical connection being established in his brain. He felt shaky and sat down on the floor in a corner all to himself as The Man's energy flowed into him, a bright red flood of it filling every corner and crevice of his being until it was as if The Man's body was covering his own like a perfect, form-fitting armour, or a super-hero's costume ...

and he felt so strong and powerful in that moment ... so wholesome and good ... so capable of great and wonderful things.

In that moment, he *became* The Man.

And then something else happened; the flow reversed, the tide ebbed and slowly drained away. Jason lay there helpless to stop it until, at last, he was empty not only of the new flood of energy, but of his own precious store of it as well. He felt burned out, wasted and utterly demoralised, despairing in the certain knowledge that he'd somehow lost the most beautiful, the most powerful thing that anyone could ever possess. He had squandered his birthright and blown his chance.

When morning came he stumbled into the winter streets lost and broken.

It took him two weeks to find his way back home.

...

On Boxing Day the orderlies organised the inmates and led them off the ward, down several long corridors and three sets of stairs to a painted concrete tunnel that reminded Jason of the ones at university — even the colour was the same— and gathered everyone in a small gymnasium with five high-placed windows on each side. A portable movie screen was set up in the proscenium of a small stage. Despite their best efforts, the orderlies couldn't settle everyone down as the lights dimmed and the movie started.

The movie was *The Nutty Professor* starring Jerry Lewis. Jason had no recollection of having seen the movie exactly one year ago, but he *had* seen it on television at home and recalled how the whole family, even his father, had killed themselves laughing at the hilarious antics of Jerry Lewis, especially the part where he mimed playing all the different instruments in the orchestra. Because of this family connection it occurred to Jason that the hospital had organized this showing in his honour. And then, just as quickly, it occurred to him that that was an absurd idea; he'd never been in this hospital and, in fact, NONE OF THIS HAD HAPPENED BEFORE.

Just like that, he knew the truth. He knew he'd been on a long strange journey. He knew that if he spoke sensibly to the woman who might be a nun, and to the doctor when next he saw him, that they would see the difference in him and know he was better and he knew that soon — he hardly dared think it — soon, he would simply be allowed to go home.

He considered his situation and remembered what his father had said the time his ship went down: *Stay calm and wait.* He took a deep breath and then another.

Stay calm and wait.

It was over. He was going to be okay. It really was only a matter of time.

...

One week after the last big revelation and a number of serious conversations with Dr. Alderdice and the nun-nurse lady, Jason Dade caught the outport bus in front of the Waterford Hospital. They would see him again as an out-patient, but for the moment, seemed to think it was a good idea for the young man to go home.

It was dark when the outport bus finally reached Birthlayn and pulled up beside the house. He stepped into the clear still night and stared up at a sky wild with stars. He quietly opened the gate and walked into the yard. The pathway and steps were neatly cleared of snow, a shovel leaned patiently against the house. The kitchen window cast its welcoming yellow glow. They were expecting him. He lifted the latch and opened the storm door with barely a sound. He stopped for a moment to embrace this last minute alone and saw through the window that a place was set for him at the table. His mother was tending to the pots on the stove.

He pushed open the inside door, stepped into the porch and slipped off his boots in the dark. The warmth of the kitchen struck him like a wave. His mother glanced up and smiled, then went back to stirring her jam with a well-worn wooden spoon. His father sat watching television in the front room.

Amongst a flood of familiar smells he caught the sweet scent of spruce drying behind the stove. He hung up his coat and sat to the place prepared for him at the table. His mother slipped a plate of hot stew in front of him and touched him on the shoulder.

That was all he needed.

Sarah was doing homework in her room.

His father spoke quietly from his chair without taking his eyes from the evening news. "Everything all right?" he asked.

Jason looked at his mother. "Everything's fine," he said, and gratefully tasted his food.

After supper Johnnie Breen came to the house. "There's a crowd skating on the pond," he said. "You want to come along?"

Jason found his skates in the usual place, hanging on a nail by the door.

...

The summer he was eight years old Jasie Dade was led one day by some secret sense to explore the woods across the road from their house. Those woods were at the top of a steep hill above George Breen's meadow and so were called George's Woods. His legs grew tired from the long climb and he hadn't quite made it to the top when a yellow bird darted out of a small spruce right at the edge of the tree line. There was alarm in her short sudden flight and he noticed she didn't stray far.

There must be a nest.

So he got down on all fours and crept into the low-lying branches and there it was, small grey twigs from a hundred flights to and fro, mud harvested from the bog above the hill, and the deft curve of straw inside a small bowl the size and shape of an eggcup; all of it safe, cool, and secure on a branch in the shadows. It contained the miracle of three tiny eggs. The smallest he'd ever seen.

He didn't mention the nest that night at supper because he didn't want to be warned away from it. When he went back the next day, the egg count had increased to four.

He visited several times that day and always found her there with her yellow-green feathers, her eye a black dot that might have been dabbed on with the tiniest of paintbrushes, sitting on the nest glaring at the intruder as he crept closer and closer until she could stand it no longer and flew away. He'd wait until she came back and, fascinated by her small fierce presence, would start the slow stalking process all over again until she flew, and he did that over and over again all day long.

On the third day, he rose again and ascended to the woods. He found the nest abandoned, the eggs cast out and broken. Guilt and confusion flooded his young heart as he turned away and stumbled down the hill. And then he was crying, running as fast as he could for home, his young legs moving faster and faster until it seemed they would outrun his body and he would fall disastrously down and not be able to get up and he knew that he could tell no one about this wrong of his, that the guilt was his to bear and that he would have to carry it in his secret heart alone until time, and only time, had done its healing work.

Acknowledgements

I am grateful for the financial support of the Canada Council for the Arts, the Newfoundland and Labrador Arts Council, and the City of St. John's.

Thanks to Joan Sullivan for permission to use lines from *The Typical Newfoundlander* by Rose Hoskins.

Further thanks to Jessica Grant, and especially, Kathleen Winter, for editorial guidance, mentorship, and support.

Paul Rowe is a writer, actor, and teacher born in Point Verde, a small coastal community on Newfoundland and Labrador's Avalon Peninsula. He has written, directed, and performed extensively during a theatre career spanning three decades. In 2015 he was a member of the acting company at the Stratford Festival. *The Last Half of the Year* is his second novel. His first novel, *The Silent Time*, was a finalist for the 2008 Winterset Award. Paul Rowe lives in St. John's.